NO SHOES,
NO SHIRT,
NO TRIAL

by
Judge Deidra Hair

Published by
SYMETRY PUBLICATIONS
Box 44177 Cincinnati, Ohio 45244

ISBN 0-9633515-0-8

Edited by

Laura Pulfer
and
M. Lynne Smith

Printed on
Politically Correct
Recycled Paper

recycled paper

Dedicated
to
Bubbles
and
Albert

Introduction by Nikki Giovanni

Table of Contents

INTRODUCTION

I've never been to jail. My sister went to jail once, for charity. The night before she was to go behind bars a startling thought occurred to her: "What if nobody bails me out?" I had to fly to San Francisco so that she would be assured of at least one person being willing to come get her. Mother thought it was the right thing to do. "Don't you think you should go to San Francisco and support your sister?" she innocently asked. I thought the air fare would be better spent sending it for the mock bail. But Mother was right. Gary did not need money at that point. She needed to know someone would be there.

I grew up in the Sixties where most of my contemporaries, in fact, did go to jail. I am not sure how or why I didn't. I sat in, I marched, I protested and yet I was never there when the paddy wagons rolled up. I suppose I was lucky in a way. I have no yearning to have gone to jail. I would like to have been with Diane Nash and John Lewis when they rolled into Mississippi. It was courage beyond courageous to know that either jail or death awaited you at the end of the Freedom Ride. But I was both scared and underage. I didn't have any true sense of death and I don't think the idea of jail was such a bother but the idea of riding Greyhound through Alabama still sits poorly with me. On my better days I like to think I'm not a coward but I'm also not quixotic, rumor to the contrary. I do like to have a chance, so when police pull me over for speeding I keep my hands in sight and generally say "Yes, Sir" and "No, Sir" on dark highways. I offer no explanation for whatever action they are querying and only once did I say to the officer: "I don't believe you." Adding "Sir" when he said "What?" "I think you are lying, Sir" I said. But that was in Hyde Park in Cincinnati at high noon. He was, by the way, lying, but I had to pay the ticket anyway. I do understand rage.

Municipal Court is, perhaps, the first and only court most of us see. We have an abusive spouse; we are drunken drivers; we rob or mug someone . . . the normal course of things humans run into in everyday life. Someone says we owe them money; our dog barks too loudly late at night; someone is peeking in our windows. Most people are not involved in the court system for social justice but rather human ineptitude. Something we should not have done or something we should have . . . a maze of rules we either ignored or did not understand.

If anything distinguishes humans, it is our ability to laugh. Judges need a sense of humor as much as an understanding of law. Perhaps law plus humor will equal justice. Your basic murder, rape, malicious wounding are clearly wrong, but television notwithstanding, most of us don't do clear crimes. Most of us do dumb, stupid, silly things that bring us into a system from which there is no escape. Once we go into the system we find ourselves still there . . . our own dumb actions keeping the juggernaut rolling. There is no real mystery to Municipal Court. For the most part, it is trying to teach us good manners: How to get along with each other, and good citizenship: How to conduct our public selves so that we are not a nuisance to our neighbors. Kindergarten is an attempt to serve the same purpose, but some of us were fidgety and never learned to put our toys away, close our eyes at naptime, eat only our own cookies and not hit each other. Municipal Court steps in when Kindergarten fails.

Judge Deidra Hair is one of the finest judges I know. She approaches her job as judge thoroughly, though with humility. Probably a reflection of the English courses she took as an undergraduate. She has the rather strange notion that justice should serve rather than just be dispensed. She also knows Art Linkletter was right: People Are Funny.

I'm delighted Judge Hair decided to share some of her experiences on the bench. We need more insight into our own behavior as humans; we also need to know how we must look sometimes to other people. I thoroughly enjoyed her reminiscing. I'm sure all of her readers will. She has taken a small light into a small space and brightened our understanding of both the court and ourselves. Bravo, Hair. It is a brave and wonderful thing that you do.

Nikki Giovanni

Chapter I
THE HOLE TRUTH AND SOMETHING BUTT

Why? Why would you order a pizza delivered to your very own house, then rob the delivery boy at gun point? If you know the answer, stop reading now and give this book to your Aunt Sadie for Christmas. If you don't know the answer, then close the bathroom door and make yourself comfortable as we ponder the daily realities of our criminal justice system.

In the court system, as in life, the whole is only as good as the sum of its parts — courts, judges, prosecutors, witnesses, defense attorneys, police, and defendants. This conglomerate, this punch-bowl mix, forms the *whole*. Reader, beware; this book is not about the whole; it is, rather, about the *hole*.

The hole is that translucent, extra–terrestrial spot in each courtroom where reason and logic float like an oil slick on the water . . . never really penetrating the water's surface. The slick moves, without warning, about the courtroom, like a sing–a–long's bouncing ball skimming the surface, just out of reach. Round and round she goes . . .

and where she stops, nobody knows. Like the Bermuda Triangle, the hole is a convenient way of explaining the inexplicable.

The hole not only sucks in people, it sucks in the law itself. An example of the hole occurred recently in my town, with a local ordinance requiring that dog owners carry a "pooper–scooper" on their daily walks. It was a simple law, requiring dog owners to bend down and scoop up their animal's excrement, placing it in a plastic bag. Failure to abide by the law was punishable by a $100 fine. Unfortunately, the law did not list an exemption for the blind and their guide dogs. The cruel vision of a blind person groping around on the ground in order to be a law–abiding citizen is more than the conscience can handle. Clearly, this was the work of the judicial hole.

As a former prosecutor, former defense attorney, and current judge, I have personally experienced the devastating effects of the hole. The hole explains why someone would order a pizza delivered to his own address, then rob the delivery person at gun point. The hole explains why a prostitute charged her client with passing a bad check. The hole explains why so many defendants confess to uncommitted crimes by saying "I axed my mother" instead of "I asked my mother." It explains why hundreds of people come to court each year to plead "No Contents" instead of "No Contest." The hole explains why some defendants, noticing the HON. DEIDRA L. HAIR sign on my bench, refer to me conversationally during their trials as "hon." The hole also explains why Billy Caudill went to jail for six months.

Billy was a career drunk driver. He had eight convictions within the prior five years, and he had never had the benefit of a driver's license. In addition to being drunk most of the time, Billy also lacked the *driving gene*. This is a gene most of us have, allowing us to drive to and from work every day without colliding with other autos, buildings, or pedestrians. Billy first became aware of his handicap when, at the age of sixteen, he drove his mother's car directly into a train stopped at a railroad crossing. The train's engineer was the first person to diagnose Billy's handicap. This railroad man had heard of people being hit by moving trains, but he had never heard of a parked train being hit by a moving car.

The absence of the driving gene wasn't Billy's only medical difficulty. His liver was the approximate size of Texas, and his doctor had advised him that continued consumption of hard liquor would kill him. Taking this suggestion under advisement, Billy did the sensible thing; he switched to beer. Not just any beer. Looking out for his health, Billy always ordered "Lite" beer.

Billy lived directly across the street from a small shopping plaza which contained a large K–Mart. On one sticky Cincinnati summer evening, Billy ran out of cigarettes. He wasn't a plan–ahead kind of guy, so he got into his car and barreled straight across four lanes of heavy traffic to the K–Mart. Billy also ran through an outdoor garden furniture display and a large plate glass window, before coming to rest in the housewares department. He just didn't see the store. It snuck up on him, as the train had years before.

At sentencing, when I asked Billy why he didn't walk across the street to the store, he responded, "Judge, I'm sorry, but I was just too damn drunk to walk." Of course, I knew better; I knew that Billy was really just another victim of the great judicial hole.

Like some television evangelists, the hole is particularly fond of the meek, the mild, the misinformed, and, above all, the terminally misguided. People just like L.A. Roy (pronounced Lee–Roy). Now, L.A. Roy was only 18 years old when he decided to pull his first big robbery. He bought a ski mask and a sawed–off shotgun and off he went to Ferd's Bar and Grill, waiting patiently until ten minutes before closing, so the cash register would be filled. He leapt from his car and stormed through the front door screaming, "This is a stick–up; give me all the money and nobody gets hurt." But, this was Ferd's Place. It wasn't Flo's Place or Edy's Place, where the ski mask robbery might have worked. On this night, like every other, Ferd was bartending. He and his patrons were sloshed to the gills. Ferd looked down the short barrel of that shotgun and said, "Get your butt out of here before I tear it off and feed it to you for breakfast." Another patron chimed in: "Yeah, let's all have a piece of that!" Sensing defeat, L.A. Roy ran back outside, as the assembled crowd cheered. During this brief episode, nobody in the bar moved. Everybody held their stool. Nobody, except L.A. Roy, panicked.

For L.A. Roy, it was a night of humiliation, but he had learned that the concept of "Victimless Crime" was not just something you read about in the newspaper. It was the night L.A. Roy met the hole. That's the hole truth . . . and something butt.

Chapter II
SYSTEMS ANALYSIS

To the ordinary person of average intelligence, the court system appears to be a maze of obscure language and insider tricks. Pavlov, in his most exquisite experiment, would have been unable to direct the rat through this legal labyrinth. Clearly, it is a creation of humans, not of God.

Now, most people, in the process of living, become at least marginally aware of the medical profession and its system. We know this because doctors make far more money than lawyers, which means that people see doctors with far greater frequency than they see lawyers. So, the best way to explain the legal system is by contrasting it with the medical system. We have come a long way from the days of the bumbling prosecutor, Hamilton Berger, and his brilliant adversary, Perry Mason. The lesson of that television show was simple. The prosecutor is *a priori* a buffoon, and the defendant is always innocent. With the exception of the William Kennedy Smith trial, nothing could be further from the truth in actual courtrooms.

The "new" truth can be seen every day through television accounts on episodes of L.A. Law,

Divorce Court, Judge Wapner and, most significantly, live Court TV. On the latter, we see the real thing. There are no stages and no actors, just real blood–and–guts cases, decided by real judges and real juries. The law, compared to medicine, is something of an exhibitionist profession. It seems unlikely, for example, that live Surgery TV is imminent. Imagine the interview with the family before surgery. Picture the interviews with the surgeon and the anesthesiologist, followed by expert commentary from a surgical instruments salesman. Imagine a panel of experts commenting on the precision of every incision or suction procedure. Imagine the tracing of the transplanted organ's history, up close and personal. Imagine the interview with the family, after the patient's death. Imagine the lawyers watching the show, searching for the slightest cause for a malpractice suit.

The real reason that live medical TV is unlikely is because the law does not require public surgery. The law does, however, require a public trial. In state courts, absent a significant and compelling reason, the judge must permit cameras in the courtroom. Federal judges do not have to follow this rule because they are appointed for life, and they don't have to do anything they don't want to do. But this results in those hilarious artists' renderings of court proceedings, which invariably make the defendant look like Dick Tracy or Jughead. In state court, the judge may limit the viewing of a witness by ordering the witness' face to be either distorted or blacked out. What would be particularly amusing would be a control panel, allowing the judge to distort the witness' nose as he/she testifies. In the law, this is known as the Pinocchio factor.

I recall one such Pinocchio case in which the defendant was charged with assaulting a woman in a bar. Asked by the prosecutor why he threw the woman, face first, into a wall, he replied: "Well, I was a little drunk . . . I thought she was a chair." A little drunk? Enter the Pinocchio distortion with the Court TV commentator's voice–over: "Well, folks, looks like the judge didn't think too much of that explanation." As live Court TV develops, it may even be possible to black out the judge's face. This would be particularly beneficial in a controversial case wherein it is likely that the judge's decision will be politically unpopular.

One other distinction between the legal and medical professions is that lawyers are far more "open" about their work. They truly want people to understand how the system works, and they want people to participate. For example, lawyers have encouraged and developed small claims courts. Often these courts are referred to as "small brains" or "small change" courts, but the fact remains that there is no equal in the medical profession. These "people's courts" are specifically designed to resolve minor civil disputes without involving lawyers. The judge or referee hears the facts, applies a little law, and a little common sense, and presto . . . a judgment.

The only other significant difference between law and medicine is that doctors are required to really practice their trade before being sent into the real world. In the medical system, it is customary to select a specialty and then complete an internship in that field. Since lawyers know it all upon graduation from law school, they are not required to specialize or to intern.

With the exception of the aforementioned differences, the legal system and the medical system are quite analogous. The emergency room (ER) in any hospital is the first stop for critical care. In the legal system, the ER is the lowest trial court. From the ER, the patient is moved into the intensive care unit (ICU). In the legal system, the ICU is the secondary trial court. Ultimately, the patient is seen in the morgue. With some patients this is a rapid journey, and with other patients it may take years. The morgue is the legal equivalent of the Court of Appeals. The lower trial courts are best viewed as massive, bloody battle grounds. As the few surviving soldiers grow weary and lay down their arms, it is the job of the Court of Appeals to run over the hill and shoot the wounded. The final step is, of course, the funeral parlor. This is the legal equivalent of a Supreme Court. It is the job of the Supreme Court to remove the gold from the teeth of the soldiers who have been the untimely victims of the Court of Appeals, and to forthwith effect a suitable burial. Mercifully, euthanasia is never permitted in the legal system.

Chapter III
LAWS 'R' US

In the layering of the court system, from the equivalent of the emergency room to the grave, we have created a system of strangely inverted judicial power. On appeal, the higher courts (Supreme and Appellate) methodically review each legal decision which is made in the lower trial courts. Their work is confined to a review of the record or transcript of the proceedings. It's a little like a "Scratch and Sniff" court because they never see, hear, or really smell the people who were involved in the case. Thus, these higher courts are not the "People's" Courts, they are the autopsy courts, where the bodies are filed away and examined on a first–in, first–out basis.

Upon the completion of every trial, the attorneys must decide if they believe that the trial judge committed an error which is so extreme that the case must be reversed. This is known as prejudicial error. Prejudicial error is a basis for a reversal of the case. For example, if you shoot into a crowd of people, and no one is hit, that is "harmless" error. But if someone is injured by your misdeed, the error becomes "prejudicial." Or, following our previously established medical/legal model, if the ER doctor accidentally leaves a tiny sponge in your stomach after surgery, this is "harmless" error. This is true because the sponge may in fact be beneficial, in that it acts as a small, but permanent, antacid implant. On the other hand, if the ER doctor mistakes your stomach for your leg, and amputates it . . . this is "prejudicial" error. Due to the overwhelming volume of cases handled by the higher courts, it takes years before a decision is published. That can be an incredible wait if you are in jail, or hobbling around on one leg.

In sharp contrast to the higher courts, the lower trial courts act immediately, with the information available at the time, and with little or no time for reflection. These are not the "research and reflection" courts. Rather, they are the "action" courts. The judges here are like the ER specialists, and like the ER doctor, they must use every method to save the patient — even if it means a slight deviation from a standard operating procedure. This actually creates an inversion of power, whereby the "lower" trial courts make all of the critical emergency decisions that truly affect the life of the patient. The higher court autopsy team can only tell us what went wrong, and how to avoid the error in the future. But, as in medicine, this is usually of no great comfort to the deceased.

Every metropolitan court system has the equivalent of an Air Care medical helicopter, which carries the patient from the scene of the accident to the ER. In the law, this is known as the General Arraignment Room. In our system, it is called simply "Room A." Every crime which occurs in the entire county is scheduled for an immediate and brief initial hearing in Room A. This often amounts to three hundred cases a day, which must be heard by a single judge. The cases include everything from letting your dog run loose to aggravated murder. This is the heart of the system, and to keep it beating often requires creativity and imagination. In the medical profession this is called genius. In the judicial profession, it is often called reversible error. But reversible error only occurs if somebody is unhappy with your decision. So, as a judge, the key to avoiding reversal is to design your innovations with happy endings.

Since no set of laws can allow for the infinite variety of human behavior, judicial creativity is a limitless exercise. My personal favorite invention is the Failure–to–Hide warrant. This theory was devised in Room A, in response to a case involving a career criminal, Elroy Watkins, charged with assaulting his neighbor, DeWitt Grubb, with a tire iron. DeWitt, not coincidentally, had been charged

with assaulting Elroy with a garden hoe on the
very same day. This was a Hatfield–McCoy script.
The players had each been in court eight times
within a six month period. Neither defendant was
convicted of anything, because no judge could
decide, beyond a reasonable doubt, who started
the fight. In one such trial, when Elroy and
DeWitt began screaming at each other in the
courtroom, I banged the gavel and said,"Stop it!
Now, you can't both testify at once. I am going to
have to insist that you lie one at a time." I didn't
intend to say that, but it slipped out. A judicial
oops or a slip of the Freudian scalpel/gavel. Bad
Judge. Bad, bad Judge.

Well, seeing Elroy and DeWitt return to Room
A so promptly brought all the past incidents to
mind. Boys will be boys, but Elroy and DeWitt had
simply gone too far. I had to try something
different, something that would keep them from
clogging our dockets, something that would
prevent their actually killing each other. I asked
Elroy what he wanted to happen to DeWitt as a
result of their latest encounter. Elroy told me that
"All I ever wanted was for DeWitt to stay away
from me, period!" When I asked DeWitt what he
wanted from the legal system, he also stated that
all he wanted was for the Court to make Elroy
stay away from him.

From such humble beginnings the "Failure–to–Hide" warrant was born. I explained to Elroy and DeWitt that I was dismissing their cases against each other, but that I was issuing a far more serious sanction. Henceforth, whenever either man saw the other, he must run and hide, and remain secreted until the coast was clear. If they were both on the same side of the street, they were to run in opposite directions and hide. At no time were they allowed to engage in verbal or other symbolic communication.

Now, clearly, the law nowhere authorizes a Failure–to–Hide warrant, even in Judge Wapner's courtroom, and it was totally unenforceable. . . but Elroy and DeWitt didn't know that, and they were happy. The system had given them just what they wanted. It worked. Since my early days on the bench, I have issued hundreds of Failure–to–Hide warrants without a single recurring incident. It became so popular that people would come in off the street and actually demand a Failure–to–Hide warrant. It had become a Constitutional right.

The pace in Room A is grueling. Three hundred cases in one day is the approximate equivalent of a fourteen–hour stint in the ER, with no assisting physicians. In this atmosphere, the court functionaries often become flat and rote. Once, hearing a commotion outside of the courtroom, I

saw some police officers charge into the hallway.
Within minutes, they returned, dangling a woman.
She was being carried from underneath her arms,
her skinny little legs kicking in the air. The county
lock–up was located behind the bench in Room A.
So, the only way to enter from inside the building
was through the courtroom. The complication was
that she was stark, buck–naked. For mysterious
reasons, she removed her clothing outside the
courtroom door and threw it all to the floor. The
police gathered it all up and began tossing it at
her, urging her to get dressed and move on. As
they threw a garment, she'd grab it and throw it
back. It was like an adolescent clothes fight.

Now, Room A is only slightly smaller than a
basketball court, so it took some time to escort her
through the crowded courtroom. I never took my
eyes off her, but I never missed a beat of the
relentless judicial drum. The case I was hearing
proceeded without hesitation. It was as if we were
all dreamers in the dream, off in our own reality of
maintaining the dignity of the court, no matter
what. I felt like screaming, "For God's sake, they
just brought a naked lady through the courtroom!"
But, unlike an episode of <u>Night Court</u>, I didn't
scream, and neither did anyone else. Perhaps this
is what people really mean by "judicial temperament."

The utter exhaustion of a Room A assignment can lead to some very strange extra–judicial solutions. For example, the reverse play "Failure–to Run–Away–Entirely" warrant. I first used this creation with a group of twenty out–of–town prostitutes.

Every year my city hosts a summer jazz festival which draws a wide and festive audience. Every year prostitutes migrate to Cincinnati in rented vans and motor homes, to take advantage of the thousands of jazz fans pouring into the city. And every year, the police round them up and hold them for the Room A docket. It's all quite ritualistic and quite predictable. Each prostitute, with the assistance of a public defender, would plead guilty and I would proceed with the sentence. I would inquire about the make, model, and license number of their vehicle. I noticed the pimps leaving the courtroom, returning with small pieces of paper listing the requested information, which would then be entered into the record.

Each prostitute received the same sentence . . . ten days in jail or leave town by 5 o'clock. I told them that the prosecutor would be on the North I–75 entrance ramp, with his clipboard, at precisely 5 p.m. In addition to that, the police helicopter, I explained, would verify their departure from the air. Of course, the prosecutor and the public defender played their roles exquisitely, remaining perfectly poker–faced throughout the hearings. To further enhance our plan, we told the defendants that they must check in with the state Highway Patrol headquarters in Dayton, Ohio, by 6:15 p.m. The Highway Patrol boys have never been known for a collective sense of humor. I don't know what ever happened to these ladies, but I do know that they were not rearrested in my jurisdiction. And, like Elroy and DeWitt, that's all I wanted from the system. But I have to chuckle every time I picture those twenty prostitutes checking into the Highway Patrol office. I also have to monitor my speed very carefully when I pass through Dayton, Ohio. I have a feeling those jovial patrol fellows would love to have a chat with me.

Failure–to–Hide warrants, Failure–to–Run–Away–Entirely Warrants . . . both are attempts to keep an already impossibly overcrowded system from overflowing. Let's face it; sometimes Laws 'R' Us.

Chapter IV
THROUGH SICK AND SIN

Like the E. R. Team, it is very important that all members of the judicial "team" work together harmoniously, toward a common goal. The Emergency Room doctor has his trusty nurse and assisting interns. The judge has his trusty bailiff, clerk, and court reporter. Unlike the nurse and her rather extensive medical training, however, the bailiff has absolutely no legal training. He is generally a political appointment, whose specialty is *getting along with people.*

I recall one newly appointed bailiff who was given a series of flash cards or cheat–sheets to indicate what he was to say and when he was to say it. His first task, as anyone who has watched Night Court knows, was to open Court, and his card read: (Rap, Rap, Rap), Please rise. This separate session of the Hamilton County Court is now in session. Please be seated and remain quiet." When he dutifully said "Rap, Rap, Rap," the need for basic training became apparent. For the remainder of his career he was known simply as "Rap–Rap the Bailiff."

My bailiff was, of course, without fault. Well, except that he ate continuously. Not that he took excessive coffee breaks; on the contrary, he didn't even sit and eat. Instead, he would pace and eat at the same time. He was especially partial to powdered sugar doughnuts. One morning he had spilled so much powdered sugar on the carpet that I could actually see his footprints in a path from his desk to mine. Every time I sent him on an errand outside the courtroom, he would return with mustard on his tie or relish on his chin. He was such a regular customer of the hot dog vendor that the hot dog push–cart was always located directly outside my courtroom. It rather added to the circus atmosphere, but it kept the bailiff happy . . . and that kept me happy. As the years passed, advances in cooking technology and the downsizing of kitchen appliances increased the amount and variety of foods the bailiff could prepare for himself without even venturing outside to the sidewalk vendor. Often, our trials would be interrupted by the muffled "ding, ding, ding" of the microwave oven in my office, mystifying most spectators, but signaling to the bailiff the completion of his latest cake, brownies, or other treat.

The court clerk is the equivalent of the hospital accountant. He is responsible for transmitting and

filing all official court records. The clerk also
collects fines and records payment. My clerk, Mr.
Red, is a former bar owner and bartender. He has
a natural ability to communicate with many of the
regular court customers. He can also do a great
"chi–ching" imitation, as he collects fine money.

The third member of the official and immediate
judicial team is the court reporter. The reporter
sits directly below and in front of the judge. The
reporter is a buffer between the defendant and the
bench. A reporter must maintain an intense
concentration on the spoken word . . . often to the
exclusion of the context of the conversation. My
first court reporter, "Slicko," had a habit of
translating testimony with her mouth open and
her eyes fixed in a drug–like trance. The more
exhausted she became, the more her mouth would
droop toward her chest.

Slicko was in just such a slack–jawed pose
when I sentenced a man to six months in jail.
Understandably, he was not pleased with the
sentence. His response was a snarled "Fuck you!"
This is known as a post–traumatic sentence
response. Well, when this happens, the judge is
obligated to hold the defendant in Contempt of
Court, and order additional jail time to be attached
to the original sentence. This is such a routine
procedure that as soon as the defendant uttered

the words, two armed bailiffs jumped to his side in anticipation of my contempt lecture.

I quickly glanced at Slicko, who was off in another open–mouthed world. "Ms. Reporter," I said, "could you please repeat what the defendant said for the record?" She snapped to attention, looked me straight in the eyes, and said, "He said, Thank you." She had absolutely no idea what had happened. The prosecutor became angry and assumed that she simply didn't want to repeat such foul language. "What's the matter with you?" he chided; "The Judge has certainly heard a lot worse." What did he mean, I had heard a lot worse? I felt like a cheap, barroom floozy who should be accustomed to every possible derogatory remark.

I told the bailiff to simply remove the defendant for his original six month sentence. But what really tickled me was the thought of this surly criminal saying "Thank you, Judge, I'd love one hundred and eighty days." I couldn't continue. I called a recess so that I could run to my chambers, close the door, and have a good laugh. I also knew that it was time for Slicko to have a little coffee. It's important that the team stick together, through sick and sin.

This spirit of team play often extends beyond our immediate judicial team, to other players in the system. Under very extreme circumstances, this spirit may even extend to the Sheriff's Department. Now, among other things, it is the duty of the Sheriff to maintain the jail in a safe and efficient manner. John Peters was an unusual challenge. He was a brilliant criminal; he had a photographic memory and he knew how to use the microfilm equipment in the public library. He memorized data on judges and other public officials and delighted in reciting biographical information. With the exception of an old attempted rape conviction, his recent offenses were all petty. When not at the public library, John lived in his car; he had no family or any other social connections.

The last time I saw John he had been arrested for criminal trespass and criminal damaging. For no apparent reason, John had gone onto the property of a local country club at 2:00 a.m., where he proceeded to relocate and redecorate the pro shop. Basically, he thought it would look better in the swimming pool. Recognizing that this was ludicrously odd behavior for a forty–two year old man, I ordered him to be committed to jail for observation and a pre–sentence psychiatric evaluation.

John's evaluation revealed that he had "an exaggerated sense of self," and that he had been seriously disturbed for eight years. He was a borderline personality, the report explained. He had come to believe that everything about his body was holy and must be preserved. So, everything must be saved. Everything. Including, but not limited to, fecal matter. To the dismay of his cellmate, John refused to use a traditional toilet. Flushing anything that had come out of his body was out of the question.

John knew that he was special because soon he was given his very own room in the jail. He began, however, to sense the disapproval of the other inmates. He was heckled as he went to the exercise room, the TV room, and the cafeteria. His cell was inspected routinely for fecal matter, so his only option was to hide it . . . elsewhere in the jail. And so he did. He hid it everywhere, giving rise to legitimate claim of cruel and unusual punishment by his fellow inmates.

It is rare to see a grown sheriff snivel, grovel, and whine (except during an election campaign), but John's case was unusual. The entire jail had become a serious health hazard. John had to be released, in the spirit of team cooperation. I think this is called a sick sacrifice play. John was no longer our problem. A moment of silence for those hard working folks in the microfilm room at the public library.

Chapter V
THE NAMES GAME

Generally, State judges are elected to the bench. I firmly believe that politics and the judiciary should never be mixed, but such is not the reality, nor is it ever likely to be in my lifetime.

It must be remembered that judges are prohibited from discussing pending cases, and may not publicly state an opinion on any matter that might conceivably come before the court. Judges can only make one campaign promise, and that is to uphold the law. So, you might ask, how do people intelligently vote for judges? Voters are interested in prospective judges' views on abortion, capital punishment, and mandatory sentencing. But judges may not answer those very basic questions. Instead, judges must act as if they have no opinions on such important matters. Now, what nitwit has no opinion on such monumental societal issues?

The astute voter must look at group endorsements to determine judicial bias. For example, was the candidate endorsed by the Fraternal Order of Police or the American Civil Liberties Union? What is the position of the

Teamsters or of the Council of Churches? If the endorsement process is examined, it is clear, to me at least, that the logic of judicial elections is farcical, at best. If a candidate is endorsed by the Pro–Lifers, doesn't that mean that the candidate is Anti–Choice? Of course, that is the precise meaning and intent of the process. The concept of the "fair and impartial" judiciary blurs. I know one judicial candidate who actually received the endorsement of the Pro–Life and the Pro–Choice factions. We can conclude, I suppose, that this candidate was either schizophrenic or extremely fair. The clever voter, then, must look for clearly conflicting endorsements in order to determine true impartiality. Perhaps a litmus test would be the dual endorsement of the Fraternal Order of Police and the Gay Alliance. But . . . this may still leave open the issue of schizophrenia, or other significant mental defects.

Since judges cannot publicly state an opinion on any subject, they are forced into the political "suck–up" game that has totally discredited American politics. Name recognition is the game, and the Media is the method. For example, one judge would volunteer to hold Court each Christmas so he could behave like Santa and do some good deed for some pathetically abandoned homeless defendant. It was as if he had overdosed on old Bing Crosby Christmas movies; he was possessed . . . but for just this one very special day of the year. The media covered the story for two years, and then lost interest. So did the judge, who, by the way, is quite likely an agnostic. But who would ever know, because he couldn't comment in public on that either.

As a fledgling judge on the campaign trail, I learned the three primary rules of politics:

1. Never wear a coat.
2. Never say "Nice to meet you."
3. Always use politically correct language.

You never wear a coat because you can't sneak out of a gathering inconspicuously if you have to rummage around for your coat. You never say "Nice to meet you." because, invariably, you have already met the person, and you will simply make them feel insignificant. Instead, you should say, "Good to see you." At least this acknowledges that you may have met before, even if in a prior life.

The proper use of politically correct language is more complicated, requiring practice. It involves taking everyday legal jargon and combining it with the word "challenged" so that the description becomes non–judgmental, neutral, fair. Above all, a judge should be fair. So, a slut, whore, or prostitute becomes, in the words of a judicial candidate, a person who is "sexually challenged." The drunken driver is "vehicularly challenged," and the wife beater is "spousally challenged." Of course, the crazier–than–a–loon, mean, drug addict is "chemically challenged." So much for the basics.

The next step for the novice is the study of proper parade decorum. As we all know, your conduct in a parade is a significant clue to your judicial temperament. For female judicial candidates, the parade is similar to being a prom queen. Your job is to sit up, straight and tall, on the back seat of an American–made convertible, smiling, waving, and creating a general excitement. The wave is critical . . . it must be slight, delicate, and close to the body. Queen Elizabeth is the proper role model here, for posture, decorum, and stylized waving.

For male judges, this endeavor is somewhat more analogous to a Homecoming parade. The convertible should be rugged (i.e., not pink) and, of course, American–made. His wife and children must be in the car. If there are no children, some must be borrowed. The male "wave" is enthusiastic. The arms are extended far from the body in a broad, sweeping motion. Great care must be used, however, so as not to expose any perspiration stains. This is true unless the parade is being held in a working–class neighborhood, in which case, the damper the better.

I participated in one parade. My prom queen days were far, far behind me. The parade was a horrible experience in politics and the judiciary, and frankly, I would have preferred a root canal. Some of my fellow judges have been equally as successful (NOT) in this primal political activity. One judge was entered in the St. Patrick's Day parade with his entire family. His car was placed directly behind the donkeys and elephants. Out of the crowd popped a drunken defendant who yelled, "Hey, Judge, you're a fag!" The crowd cheered the drunkard on, and the donkeys and elephants did what came so naturally . . . and in such large quantity. Before the judge knew it, his hand was extended to the crowd, with the middle finger slightly elevated in the universal gesture of contempt. He had given new definition to the concept of "judicial restraint." His second parade ended equally ignominiously, when his car broke down and he was towed backwards through the entire parade route.

My first campaign is the one that brings my fondest memories. There were no women then on the bench in our county. I had been blessed with a very creative and energetic campaign chairman. Our first task was to formulate a catchy campaign slogan. We studied judicial jingles that had been successful in prior elections. Perhaps the best

example was: "Judge Smith . . . Firm, but Fair."
Wow, that said it all, but it had already been used.
We thought the slogan "Arbitrary and Capricious"
would amuse too few, while "Vote for Judge Hair . . .
a Judge with Convictions" might confuse too many.
The latter slogan was almost irresistible, but basic
good taste prevented me from engaging in
jingle–justice. Ultimately my slogan was "Judge
for Yourself." We encouraged people to call and
make an appointment to spend a day on the bench
with me. The idea was a huge success; often people
would call to make multiple appointments. I think
it's a good process and it's one I have continued.

Once a slogan had been decided upon for that
first campaign, I took to the streets to meet and
greet "The Electorate." Another primary rule of
politics is that the candidate must always carry
some small gift, or handout, with his or her name
printed boldly on the surface. Nail files, fans,
pencils, and cheap combs are extremely popular
with the political in–crowd. My selection was a
small, cheap note pad with the phrase "Keep
Judge Hair" prominently displayed on the front
cover. Like every other politician, I would attend
labor picnics and church festivals with a crew of
loyal friends and campaign workers. But my
favorite stump was in front of the I.G.A. grocery
store in my own neighborhood. During that first

election, I had lived in the neighborhood for twenty years and knew most of the locals. I felt certain that they would vote for me; after all, they were like family.

On one chilly, late October morning, I was posted at my I.G.A. stump when I spotted an elderly, dapper gentleman exiting the store. I greeted him with a smile, a note pad, and my usual request: "I hope you'll remember to vote in November." He smiled and looked at the note pad.

He then patted me on the shoulder and said, "Don't worry, honey, I've voted for him every year so far."

Well, what the heck, every vote counts. But I know there's got to be a better way.

Chapter VI
THE H.S.I. DEFENSE

In the seventies, female lawyers were an enigma, something of a freak of nature. Because trial work was viewed as aggressive and unladylike, most women who finished law school practiced outside the courtroom. The only socially acceptable trial work for attorneys who happened to be women was domestic relations or juvenile justice. After all, women were best suited to deal with other irrational women and bad, bad children. This attitude was so accepted that it was openly discussed in court.

In my first month as a prosecutor, I was assigned to the trial of a grandmother–shoplifter. The scene of this trial was particularly dismal. The stuffy, windowless courtroom was the size of an average kitchen. My table was within ten feet of the jury box, which was elevated three feet from the floor of the rest of the room. I arrived early so I could pick the table directly in front of the jury. I knew the importance of eye contact; we learned that early in law school. The jury filed in and looked down at me as I sat with my large, yellow legal pad. I was nervous and frankly, I did not have the best case in the world.

Grandma was sixty–two years old with tightly curled silver blue hair. She had somehow placed two toddler clothing outfits in her handbag, inadvertently, of course. In this particular courtroom, the attorney's lectern was the open stick type, with only a slanted board at the top. The jury could see my every movement, and there was no way to disguise the motions of my lower body. I have always been partial to those totally enclosed podiums, because I could take off my high heels and no one could see my feet. There was a sense of security there, of protection, and comfort. The room was so small that the podium had to be placed directly behind my chair as I faced the jury. The jurors were forced to look down at me as the defense council asked his questions directly over my head.

Grandma's defense attorney was a good–old–boy with a Sam Ervin approach. But under this courtly exterior was a man I suspected shot and killed small animals for sport. In the process of voir dire, or jury selection, defense counsel asked the first prospective juror if he would be prejudiced in favor of the prosecution because I was a woman. I should have objected, but I let it go because I wanted to hear the answer. I sat pitifully in my chair, attempting to play on the sympathy of the jurors. I thought to myself, "Surely some of them have daughters who want to be lawyers when they grow up . . . they'll like me . . . they'll be on my side."

The first juror said he thought he could be fair. The fact that I was a woman would not sway his decision. The second prospective juror answered similarly, but I sensed that he thought the question was foolish. As the proceedings continued, I could tell from their faces that the jurors were with me on this issue. They rolled their eyes and sighed with exasperation during any and all questioning dealing with my gender. They were as offended by the question as I was embarrassed.

I sat primly in my chair and began to write a brief note to the defense counsel. The jurors watched closely as they shared in my humiliation. With a flourish, I tore the paper from the pad. Every eye focused on me as I folded the paper tightly. Looking straight toward the jury, I handed the note to defense counsel over my right shoulder. He took the note from my hand and continued his questioning, but I could hear him unfolding the note as he spoke. The jury could see him unfolding the note. Within seconds, the entire jury was laughing; clearly, they were laughing at defense counsel. It was not a little titter or snicker. It was, rather, a big waa–ha belly laugh. One juror was laughing so hard she had to put her head in her hands.

The Judge, however, was not laughing. He excused the jurors and called defense counsel and me into his chambers, with the court reporter. I knew this was not going to be a pleasant, chummy social affair, nor was it his normal coffee break.

My note had been simple. It said, "YOUR FLY IS DOWN."

Apparently, the defense counsel reacted immediately by looking at his pants and groping at his fly, thus causing the swell of laughter from the jury box. My only regret was that I did not see this chain of events; I was too busy innocently gazing at the jury.

To say that the judge was not amused is an understatement. "Ms. Prosecutor," he began, "if you ever pull a stunt like that again, I will hold you in contempt and declare a mistrial." "But Judge," I replied, "that's not fair." He immediately sputtered "Fair? Fair? Fair is a circus that comes to town once a year and you missed it!" "But, Judge," I said, casting aside years of legal training, "he started it."

This was the beginning of my adult experience with the HE STARTED IT (HSI) defense. As a judge, I have found the HSI defense to be effective in approximately forty percent of all cases. It is a short leap of faith from the HSI defense to the S.O.D.D.I. (pronounced (Saudi) defense. The SODDI defense is that "Some Other Dude Did It." This defense should be raised only when the HSI defense has failed. I have often wondered if it would be possible to reduce all laws to simple childhood phrases and excuses. I know that on those days when your fly is down, in a system still so overwhelmingly male, it makes perfect sense. Chances are, HE STARTED IT.

Chapter VII
A CRIME OF FASHION

In law school, we were taught that our appearance was critical. We were taught the "psychology" of courtroom attire. Men were told to wear a navy suit, white shirt, and a reddish–maroon tie. In recent years, that outfit would be described as the classic power suit, but when I was in law school the navy suit was supposed to convey a sense of serenity, and the white shirt a sense of truth. The reddish–maroon tie purportedly made women jurors feel secure because it reminded them of their menstrual cycle. A curious notion, I thought, but then the psychologists of the sixties also thought that Timothy Leary was, in fact, alive. For reasons that may be self–evident, a trial lawyer should never, ever, wear brown. As the only woman in my law school class, I was never quite certain what to wear. I suppose that may be why I am a Judge today . . . black is so easy.

In my early years as a prosecutor, I learned that I must not only be mindful of my own attire, but I must also carefully prepare the wardrobes of my witnesses. In one sexual imposition case, I had the opportunity to interview the victim before trial. She appeared in my office in jeans and a sweatshirt and I told her to wear a simple skirt and a blouse with a high collar to court. She appeared on the day of trial in a ruffled, high–collared blouse and a mini–skirt the size of a dishtowel. She was no slave to fashion. She was also no slave to basic neuro–function. She assumed the witness stand, crossed her legs, revealing a total lack of underwear. Three members of the jury smiled and began to stare at the floor. I had told them, in my opening statement, that the defendant had forcibly fondled the victim's breasts. I had told them that it was against her will and without her consent. I was digging my own grave with a shovel, and she came to help with a backhoe. I could have asked her why she forgot to wear underwear, but the principal lesson of law school is never to ask a question for which you do not already know the answer. The case was lost in record time. As the jury was deliberating, I took the opportunity to ask the question. She explained to me that she had contacted a painful case of shingles and couldn't tolerate even the slightest pressure on her skin. Her doctor had advised her not to wear any underwear, and to stay at home attired only in a lightweight muumuu or shift. To this day, she is angry with "the system" and I have to agree; it didn't work for her.

When I was a defense lawyer, I usually told male defendants to dress for court as if they were attending the funeral of a very close friend who just happened to be a priest. Defendants, however, are often an equal mix of the pathetic and the bizarre and the courtroom becomes a large Waring blender. Sammy Hall was just such a mixture.

As a young man, Sammy had it all — a wife, a home, and two daughters. He had a respectable job and a bright future. Unfortunately, Sammy's wife fell in love with another man and, according to Sammy, she up and left town with everything he had, including the children. Sammy started drinking, which became his only hobby for forty years. But Sammy wasn't a mean drunk; he was a kind soul, who was homeless and penniless as he approached his sixty–third birthday. All he wanted was to see his children before he died, but Sammy had no idea how to locate the girls. After a particularly rough encounter with a bottle of Ripple wine, God told Sammy to commit a crime that would make him famous; then when his children saw his photo, Sammy and the Ripple reasoned, they would come for him.

Sammy's plan was simple: he would rob a bank. No one would be hurt and, if it didn't work,

Sammy would go to jail, a far better fate than continuing to live on the streets, penniless and hungry. Sammy went to the drug store and purchased a set of pink hard plastic women's hair rollers. Sammy then stuffed cotton in the open end of the rollers, which were about an inch in diameter, and placed pipe cleaners into the cotton. The pipe cleaners became the wicks for the roller bombs. Attaching the bombs to his shirt with black electrical tape, Sammy put on his overcoat, and proceeded to the bank. He approached the teller and throwing his coat open to reveal the roller bombs, he handed her a note that read: GIVE ME ALL THE MONEY AND TELL MY CHILDREN WHERE I AM. The teller, predictably, sounded the bank's silent alarm and handed Sammy $5,000 in a package laden with a time–release red dye packet. The police responded immediately, knocking Sammy to one side as they crashed through the bank's front door. Sammy didn't look like a bank robber; he was too old and was in no great hurry to leave. He finally wandered off, walking one block to a bus stop and catching a bus for the center of town. The dye exploded in the back of the bus, and Sammy simply distributed the money to all the passengers. The bus driver alerted the police and Sammy was apprehended at the next stop.

This entire episode was an embarrassment — to the police, to the bank, and to the passengers who had accepted the money from Sammy. Sammy didn't make the front page and his daughters never contacted him. The only part of the plan that worked as intended was that Sammy went to jail.

As a lawyer and now, as a judge, I think I have seen it all when it comes to dress. One defendant appeared in court for sentence on his fourth drunk driving charge wearing a MILLER LITE t–shirt and a marijuana beltbuckle. The tattoo on his right arm read, "Free Drugs, Free America." His left arm bore the slogan, "Up Yours." If simple stupidity were a crime, the death penalty would have been too lenient. Simple stupidity should be distinguished from a substantial lapse from due care, or true mistake, or inadvertence. For example, I recall the public defender who appeared on a soliciting prostitution charge and sat through the entire hearing with his fly down. This was a substantial lapse from due care. But the greatest lapse occurred in the privacy of his own bathroom when he selected the neon pink underwear as his garb of the day. Justice appears as a sightless lady and the reason has become very clear to me.

The courtroom of the 1990s is often a place of high fashion. If you use and deal drugs, and support yourself on general relief, the appropriate outfit consists of exactly the clothing worn by most rap artists and imitated by most high school students of the 1990s — a black Raiders jacket, a black leather baseball cap (worn backwards), several hundred dollars worth of gold jewelry, designer pants (often black leather), and $200 running shoes. I, of course, am old enough to remember when white was the only acceptable color on the tennis court and ladies wore hats and gloves to go shopping downtown.

In any case, failure to adhere to the standard attire of the 1990s indicates that you are merely a tasteless buffoon and quite likely not the dangerous drug king–pin the prosecutor portrays. The down side is that it may also indicate that you are so dumb and tasteless that you may accidentally shoot an innocent passerby instead of the opposing drug dealer who is your target, or simply that these are the only dressy clothes you own. All of these things must be considered by the judge at the time of sentence. This is the reason that justice is blind. That lady has taste.

Chapter VIII
NO SHOES, NO SHIRT — NO TRIAL

Court appearance is not limited to issues of fashion. Appearance is your overall *persona*. For example, for a sentencing hearing, many attorneys suggest that the defendants bring all of their children to court. Babies and toddlers are particularly effective. And it is very important that all other family members remain at home. Invariably, defense counsel will tell the judge that the defendant is the sole support of these unfortunate children, and that mercy demands a light sentence or probation, thus allowing the model parent to remain in the home. This entire exercise is conducted to soften even the most heartless judge, and to raise a very practical question for the court. What is the judge going to do with a courtroom full of drooling babies after mom or dad is hauled off to jail? This trick is particularly effective with the new or inexperienced judge. When asked why the defendant has the children in court, the answer is almost always "Judge, I can't afford a baby sitter." Here it's my responsibility to wonder who was baby sitting at two o'clock in the morning while you were smoking crack and looting a convenience store? I have never heard an acceptable response.

During my first year as a judge, I often thought of banning children from the courtroom entirely. This is a drastic step for an elected official, but the final straw came when I observed a mother changing a diaper in the front row of my courtroom. Both appearance and odor revealed that the diaper was clearly full, and yes, she left it on the seat following her trial. That was it. The next day, I posted a sign by my door which read, NO CHILDREN IN THE COURTROOM. Within two weeks, defendants began appearing in those graphic t–shirts that simply say BABY across the chest with an arrow pointing to the navel area. Even the best signage has its limits.

Over the years I have experimented with various signs on my courtroom door. One read: No Shoes, No Shirt, NO TRIAL. I must admit that this had no effect whatsoever on the courtroom regulars, but it certainly made me feel that I was protecting the image of the court. My favorite sign, however, read: PLEASE CHECK ALL WEAPONS WITH THE BAILIFF UPON ENTERING THE COURTROOM. For me, it was something akin to an IQ test. Now, what damn fool would walk into a courtroom and confess that he is carrying an assault rifle under his coat? Contrary to all reason, however, within the week, my bailiff had collected three knives, one ice pick, one straight razor, and a pair of brass knuckles — and these came from the witnesses. Due to our limited weapon–storage capacity, this sign was abandoned . . . but I think of it often.

It is as important for the attorney to control the client as it is for the judge to control the courtroom. This is accomplished in varying degrees and styles. I recently heard a plea of guilty to assault of a police officer and disorderly conduct while intoxicated charges, wherein the public defender stated in mitigation of sentence, "Judge, my client is a late–stage alcoholic. He suffers from blackouts occasioned by his heavy consumption of alcohol. He is truly sorry that the officer suffered a broken nose as a result of this incident. He has absolutely no memory of this unfortunate occurrence." As his attorney was speaking, the defendant began to raise his hand up and down as if he were in grade school. He wanted my attention. He wanted to clarify the record. "Judge," he said, "I do remember some of the evening . . . I'll never forget what that rotten bastard did to me while I was drunk."

Some clients are very difficult to control. Often this is due to a mental illness or disability. Then

the judge is called upon to determine the
competency of the defendant at the time of his
initial appearance. General, or gross, competence
is determined when the defendant is aware of the
roles of his/her attorney, the prosecutor, and the
Judge. I recently asked a defendant if he
understood the role of his defense attorney and he
responded that the lawyer's job was "to get all his
money before he went to jail." The role of the
prosecutor, he said, was "to dress real neat and
then run for another office." When I asked the role
of the Judge, he responded, "I'm crazy but I'm not
stupid, and I refuse to answer that kind of
question." On the basis of his first two answers, I
had to find the man competent. In the law, truth is
always a defense.

Issues of competency are often dreadfully
intertwined with issues of alcoholism and/or just
dumber–than–a–rock stupidity. Often, it is bizarre
behavior that gets someone arrested, causing the
court to have to examine someone's actions and
determine the line between say, consumer
advocacy, acting out, and illegality. Perhaps an
example will illustrate the complexity that a mix of
alcohol and idiocy can cause. One defendant, while
shopping for denture cream at a SuperRx
drugstore, paused ever so slightly at the candy rack
and relieved himself. Upon questioning, after his

rather immediate arrest, he offered the explanation that his last Snickers bar didn't contain enough peanuts. The store officials, who claimed that the defendant ruined $60.00 worth of candy, naturally did not see this action as legitimate consumer protest. Before the trial, I asked the defendant the general competence questions. His answers were generally unremarkable, but to determine his orientation, I asked him who was President of the United States. Without hesitation, he answered, "George Bush." I recessed his trial for lunch and resumed one hour later. When the defendant returned to the courtroom, he appeared somewhat agitated and disoriented. Again, I asked him to name the U.S. President. He replied, "Judge, if you can't even remember what I just told you, I don't think I want you to hear my case."

Yes, he was competent, but he was also very drunk. As it turned out, that was exactly the problem on that fateful day at the SupeRx. No matter how you look at it, $60.00 worth of candy translates into one heck of a dousing. After years of shabbiness, my courtroom had recently been redecorated, and fearing a recurrence of his protest, I continued his trial to give him time to sober up. Never again would I confuse "competence" and "continence."

Chapter IX
NOW, WHAT DAMN FOOL...?

If there is one concept that is universal in the law, it is the "Now, what damn fool" rule. This rule applies to criminal and civil law equally and without discrimination. It is the *sine qua non* of the legal system. The concept itself, of course, dates back to the English Common Law, but it is a timeless and eternal truth. My most recent encounter with the rule occurred at my local self–service gas station. I was in a hurry, as usual, and I was out of gas, as usual. So I went to the pay–before–you–pump window and gave the attendant my $5. Thereupon I returned to my car, got in, and drove away. The next morning when I noticed the tank was still empty, I realized that I had forgotten to pump my gas the night before. I could have gone right back to the station and told the attendant that I forgot, but somehow it didn't seem plausible. Besides that, there is always a line at the pay–before–you–pump window, so other people would be listening. I just didn't have the nerve — but I have come to admire those who do.

I once heard a civil case in which the plaintiff was suing the defendant for fraud in the sale of real estate. The plaintiff (AKA the Damn Fool) had inspected the house on three separate occasions prior to the signing of the purchase agreement. Mercifully, there were no real estate agents involved in the transaction. On each inspection, the Damn Fool observed approximately two feet of water in the basement. A small canoe sat in the water, attached by ropes directly in the center of the room. Aside from this oddity, the small cinder block house was in excellent condition.

The defendant (AKA Damn Foolee) was a young, single, athletic man devoted to body building and other sporting activities. His dining room contained nothing but Nautilus equipment and assorted workout paraphernalia. Now, the Damn Fool prospective home purchaser was not stupid; he knew it was not normal for two feet of water to be in a basement. So, he asked the Damn Foolee, the athletic home owner, what caused the accumulation of water. The Foolee explained that he was training for a triathlon and that he practiced his canoeing techniques in the basement. The Foolee promised to drain the water prior to the transfer of title, which he did.

Approximately one month after the Damn Fool moved in, the basement once again filled with water. This was caused by two factors. First, the house had been built on a natural spring. Second, there was a crack in the foundation which allowed the spring water to percolate throughout the basement whenever it rained. It was not a problem that could be fixed by a waterproofing company or anyone else. The Damn Fool had a choice. Either he could take up canoeing, or he could take up court. He opted for the latter. But what is truly admirable is that the Damn Fool had the nerve to tell this whole watery story to a group of total strangers in a court of law. As the reader can easily see, I probably would have taken the coward's way out, lived with the watery basement, taken up canoeing or bought some ducks, and never mentioned it to anyone publicly.

For reasons I have yet to fathom, there is something special about water that brings out the best in the Damn Fool personality. In our county, some courtrooms are located directly below some jail cells. It has always been something of a jail house sporting event to clog the cell toilet with newspapers and flush continually until the water soaks through to the courtroom below. Of course, it's not likely that someone can get away with this prank, because, let's face it, there's only one person in each cell and he isn't going anywhere. On one such occasion, the judge simply continued the docket beneath an umbrella, as the water streamed onto the bench. Sometimes it's just not clear who is the Damn Fool and who is the Damn Foolee.

The ability to recount Damn Fool experiences and encounters with a straight face is an especially important skill in the courtroom. In the law, we call this *credibility*. Take the case of Rick "The Jogger" Bossert. Rick was arrested for jogging around a city park without his pants. According to the police, Rick drove to the park attired in a pair of runner's shorts and a T–shirt. He exited his car and ran for approximately one quarter of a mile. He then paused behind some bushes and removed his pants, continuing his run through a wooded area where he was forthwith arrested by the park police.

Rick took the witness stand in his own Damn Fool defense. With a perfectly innocent and straight face, he told me that he had been forced to remove his pants in order to "air" his hemorrhoids. To continue running without "airing" them was, Rick maintained, far too painful. Unfortunately, it was Rick's second conviction for "airing," but I was certainly touched by the novelty of his defense. I know these healthy, outdoor types don't like drugs or chemicals, but Preparation H is hardly a mood–altering substance.

I bet Rick would have gone to the pay–before–you–pump attendant and gotten his money back.

Chapter X
THE EXTRA MILE

There are some extraordinary people in life who go the extra mile, tote the extra barge, and lift the extra bale. To the untrained eye, they may appear to be carrying more of life's burdens than they should. To the trained eye, they may appear to be committing more of life's little blunders than they should. These driven folk are the *Type A* personalities whom psychologists love to write about. They are persons so driven by a purpose and meaning for life that they make the rest of us look transparent and weak, like Jello–people. It's easy to spot these folks because they walk through plate glass windows and screen doors, without so much as a single drink. They are so captured by the moment, so intent upon the task, and/or so driven by success, that even when they hit the glass door they keep going. The rest of us bounce back or simply fall to the floor, but these folks keep on going. They are, in most other ways, very bright and imaginative. They even anticipate that they or their other *Type A* friends will walk through closed doors.

In their houses you will find little decals on all the sliding glass doors, and prophylactic aluminum on the bottom of all the screen doors. Of course, in the abstract, they know that a square or rectangular hole in drywall usually signals that a window or door is present, but they seem so captivated by the moment that the abstract fades into a much larger "goal."

I had a neighbor who once walked through his sliding screen door while on his way to his back yard grill. At the time, he was carrying a platter full of hot dogs and hamburger patties. Since he was carrying the plate in front of him, it hit the screen first, but he proceeded anyway, focused on feeding his guests, undaunted, clear through the screen door. He landed face down on the patio floor, to the surprise and entertainment of the assembled guests. He had lived in that house for eight years. He knew the door was there. He also knew, at least in the abstract, that the chance it would be closed at any given time was somewhat higher than fifty per cent. But, he was overcome by the "goal" and driven by the urgency of his task. He was a true *Type A* personality.

This affliction is not limited to the corporate board room or the backyard patio. These folks are proportionately represented in the criminal world as well. For example, the most common defense to a drunk driving charge is, "I had to drive because my buddy was too drunk to do it." The buddy too drunk (BTD) defense is never successful, but it is perhaps the most common excuse offered in our criminal justice system. The goal here is to get home — not to get home safely, without injuring others — just to get home.

Mell Suggs was severely afflicted with the *Type A* personality disorder. Arrested for drunk driving, Mell was taken to a suburban police department for a breathalyzer test. He failed miserably and was given a citation for driving under the influence. The police officer told Mell to make a phone call and obtain a ride home from the station. As the police officer listened, Mell placed the call. "Emma," he began, "I'm in trouble; come and get me at the police station." What the officer couldn't hear was the other side of the conversation, which was "You're not kidding, you rotten son of a bitch . . . you were supposed to be here two hours ago!" CLICK.

As the officer completed the paper work on Mell's arrest, Mell was excused to go outside and wait for the elusive Emma. Instead, Mell went outside and took a police car left idling while another officer delivered a prisoner. Within minutes, Mell was apprehended and charged, for a second time, with D.U.I. This time he was also charged with auto theft.

By the time Mell got to court, he had filed for a divorce from Emma, the troublemaker. According to Mell, this whole unfortunate incident was all her fault. If she had just come to the police station, Mell reasoned, none of this would have happened. "Judge," Mell said, "I had to get home. I mistook that cop car for a taxi." Well, I guess he had a point. That police car was right outside the door, it was running, it had its lights on, and it had a bubble on the top. To the *Type A* criminal personality, who "just had to get home," it was as close to a taxi as it needed to be.

Chapter XI
THE RIGHT TIME AND THE RIGHT CASE

Oh boy, that was an exciting day. I was to meet my new prosecutor, the latest member of our courtroom family, a person with whom I would work for some time. My anticipation dimmed when he appeared — the shortest man I had ever met, with all the liabilities of shorthood, so perfectly captured in Randy Newman's song, "Short People." He was more than vertically–challenged; he was personality–challenged in a way that in turn challenged all with whom he worked. He inspired a deep regret that human mothers do not, on occasion, eat their young. With precisely that thought in mind, I nicknamed the little legal hors d'oeuvre Munchie.

Munchie had a very special knack for getting into trouble, all by himself. He needed no sidekick, no accomplice. No one ever had to help him, and no one ever did. One sunny day, while on his solitary lunch hour stroll, he decided to purchase a newspaper. He inserted 35 cents into the vending machine slots, bent over the machine, opened the door, and grabbed a paper. The spring–loaded door slammed shut on his securely anchored tie, yanking his face to within a few inches of the machine. Munchie was without additional change and, as usual, friendless. Even in this precarious situation, Munchie demonstrated an air of mental and moral superiority that must be the result of years of ignoring abuse and ridicule. His peers nonchalantly passed him by without a single offer of help, concern, or consolation. After about five minutes of concentrated passers–by, Munchie was freed by a businessman who wanted to buy a paper. Munchie growled to the inadvertently benevolent stranger, "Watch out, that damn machine will swallow you." Nothing was ever Munchie's fault. It was always the fault of an inanimate object possessed by an evil and retributive spirit.

My first legal encounter with the diminutive Munchie set the stage for our future relationship. Sure, he was new, but what sadistic soul would prosecute a 75 year–old widow for allowing her so–called vicious dog to run loose and bite a ten year old boy on the leg? The bite required no medical attention, and, as the facts unfolded, it appeared that the boy had released the dog from its own yard and then tormented the dog until it tried to bite him.

To illustrate her case, the widow brought the

dog to court. In human years, Wayne, AKA Vicious, was 85, nearly blind, and suffering from a hip disorder that forced him to walk in circles. The widow testified that Wayne was so feeble that she had to carry him outside to "piddle," spreading his legs for him because whenever he lifted a leg on his own, he fell down. Wayne had lost all of his teeth, accounting for the lack of medical expenses on the part of the ten year old victim. Munchie insisted on prosecuting this case and many others just like it. Being beaten in court by a toothless, crippled dog never seemed to affect him. Munchie wasn't stupid; he was just plain mean . . . and arrogant. I hoped that someday, somehow, he would mellow as he became more experienced and less threatened.

I recall thinking one day that I was a witness to the glorious transformation. Closing a lengthy drunk driving trial, he cited a case which, according to him, was factually identical to the one I had just heard. In the law, we call this "precedent." Precedent is that body of law which must be followed, and which generally forbids any original judicial thinking. Not following precedent, on a regular basis, tends to guarantee a judge a competency rating somewhere in the category of Bozo.

I was dazzled by Munchie's ability to find and cite a case exactly on point. I felt inadequate.

Surely I should have been familiar with this case; thus, I had a new respect for the miniature prosecutor. No matter how many stupid objections he made, I promised myself that I would no longer threaten to drop–kick him down Central Parkway. And yes, the dwarf–toss was ruled out. He wasn't really that short after all.

Later, I went to the Law Library and read the complete text of Munchie's precedent. To my horror, the case he'd cited had nothing to do with drunk driving, but dealt with a plaintiff suing the manufacturer of a lawn mower after running the machine over his own foot. (I've always wondered how people run over themselves with lawnmowers. Yet another application, I suspect, of the Now . . . What Damn Fool? Rule.)

Anyway, the bottom line was that Munchie had cited a case of absolutely no relevance. Whether it was deliberate or accidental, it was not to be forgotten or forgiven. A payback was clearly in order. Mercifully, the defendant would have been convicted with or without Munchie's precedent. Sleep comes so much easier knowing that the innocent, with or without their lawn mowers, are not overcrowding our jails.

For weeks, I waited for the right time and the right case for revenge. My patience was rewarded when I saw a jury trial on my morning docket for a case in which a man was charged with public indecency. The facts of the case were quite common. Every spring, our local police department conducts what can only be termed a *round–up*. Police officers are dispatched to the restrooms of our public parks to arrest men who are engaged in soliciting sexual activity. Many of these cases involve married men, with families and responsible jobs in the community. Many are deeply involved in local churches as well. It has always seemed somewhat irreverent to refer to these cases as "weeny wavers," but I suppose it fairly summarizes the offense. In this instance, our defendant was just such a fellow. He could afford the best legal defense money could buy and he intended to fight his case to the finish.

Munchie's case depended upon whether the jury believed the arresting officer. This officer had something of a career in men's rooms, and he made an excellent witness, soft spoken, articulate, exact, without an apparent chip on his shoulder or an ax to grind. But, more important, he had a sense of humor and an extreme dislike for the sniveling Munchie.

Little Munch was delighted with his case, an opportunity to destroy the defendant's life. This was the Muncher's equivalent of a runners' high. Light perspiration dotted Munchies' face as he outlined the evidence for the jury in his opening statement. "Ladies and Gentlemen," he intoned, "what you will hear today will sicken you, as it sickens me. The defendant is charged with recklessly exposing his private parts in a manner that was likely to be viewed by, and to affront, others." He droned bombastically through the hot, humid June morning.

By afternoon, the arresting officer began his testimony. His recall was surgically precise. "Officer," Munchie directed, "describe your meeting with the defendant for the ladies and gentlemen of the jury." In his best soft but still military voice, the officer responded: "I entered the men's room at six p.m. and I made eye contact with the defendant. The defendant placed his left hand on his crotch area and began what appeared to me to be a vertical motion. The defendant slowly moved toward my location and approached to within a foot of me. He then took my right hand and placed it in the location of his private parts, while making a vertical motion. I realized at that time that his pants were unzipped, and that he was exposed. I immediately called for back–up officers, and completed the arrest."

As a rule, judges rarely interfere with the examination of a witness, particularly in the presence of the jury. It is done sparingly and with the purpose of clarifying the evidence. Mindful of this, I stated in my most deliberate, judicial tone, "Mr. Prosecutor, please approach the witness and Officer, if you wouldn't mind, could you demonstrate, with the Prosecutor's assistance, what you saw the defendant do? I think it would be of assistance to the jury."

The jury strained forward, watching intently in anticipation of the scene as it was to be reenacted by Munchie and his new, close, personal friend. Through a lack of experience or common sense, Munchie did precisely as he was directed. Upon completion of his demonstration, I put my hand over my mouth, smiled uncontrollably, and thanked him for his assistance.

Very, very briefly, I felt the guilt that allows absolute power to corrupt absolutely. Then I remembered the "vicious" Wayne, tortured until he gummed his victim, and I smiled again, for the widow who wasn't there and for all the others Munchie had treated so callously, with the hope that Munchie would never again mistake a lawn mower for a drunk driver.

Chapter XII
SECURITY, WITHOUT THE BLANKET

Our county is not what you would call on the cutting edge of court security technology. Most active participants in the criminal process are violent and/or on drugs, and often carry designer weapons. Mentally–challenged individuals comprise about twenty per cent of the typical courtroom audience. Since somebody wins and somebody loses in almost every case, it's fair to say that fifty percent of the "patrons" of the court are angry at any given moment. The judges have requested metal detectors for years, but the county commissioners insist that the cost is prohibitive. Besides, judges are protected by police officers who are witnesses, and an armed bailiff who escorts prisoners to and from the jail. Personally, I would rather have a mental detector than a metal detector at my courtroom door.

My first <u>serious</u> death threat came after my first year as a judge. Before that, I had received a handful of amateur threats that could not be considered truly <u>serious</u>. For example, one defendant wrote that he intended to kill me in a most unpleasant manner, then signed the note with his full name and address. He was doing time for stealing and forging checks after a bank teller had asked him for his identification and he handed her a prison I.D. card. Clearly, this moron was a threat only to himself.

Threats made in the courtroom are fairly common and not particularly frightening because how dangerous can it be when you control all the guns? The proper legal remedy is a charge of contempt. Once my docket was interrupted by a new judge who was obviously shaken. Following sentencing, a defendant had shaken his fist at him and said, "I'll get you, you fat bastard!" This particular judge had never held anyone in contempt so he called a recess and ran over to me for advice. "Big deal," I said, "what do you expect the guy to say after you give him six months in jail? Besides, he didn't say you were a fat, OLD bastard. Now that's contempt."

Periodically, the county demonstrates some concern for the safety of judges. After a rather gruesome assassination of a judge in another state, the county ordered that the judges' benches be lined with ten inches of concrete. This, of course, forces the gunman to shoot you in the head. Frankly, I prefer the total body target, but no one asked me or any other judge. These

benches are also equipped with a "panic button"
much like those in banks, which summons the
entire sheriff's department.

I have never used this button because, when a
fight breaks out, I am the first one to run — into
my chambers. Once, a prisoner took the guard's
gun and fired it into the courtroom. The presiding
judge suffered third degree burns on his knees, but
he certainly didn't stop long enough to push that
panic button. He taught us all that rapid crawling
in a robe is a difficult but not impossible athletic
endeavor. For me, escape would have been even
more cumbersome, because of my fluffy Mickey
Mouse slippers. But, that's another story. The
crawling incident triggered a memo from the
Court Administrator:

MEMORANDUM

TO: All Judges
SUBJECT: STUN GUN

This is to advise you that the Court has
purchased a STUN GUN for use, when
necessary, to temporarily immobilize persons whose conduct is such that it disrupts
courtroom proceedings.

If you have a requirement to have this device available in your courtroom for a particular case, please contact my office.

It is recommended that all prospective users of the device read the instructions for use prior to any attempt to use it.

WOW! My very own stun gun . . . the applications seemed unlimited. If the bailiff didn't behave — or if the lawyers were getting on my last nerve — or when the witnes was telling a lie that wouldn't be believed by a preschooler — ZAP! Well, actually, I've never used the stun gun. I'm no good at anticipating the kind of craziness that would make it useful, and I have never been a read–the–directions–first kind of person. But I have used the stun gun, adroitly, in my dreams.

The most serious threat to my life came to me indirectly, through our local police. A woman who had been beaten by her husband reported him to the police, told them her husband, a glue sniffer, was very high. Taking his gun, she reported, he was on his way to the courthouse "to kill that bitch." As there were two female judges, I of course assumed it was the other bitch who had captured his admiration. But when the police traced his name and criminal record, we discovered he was

mine, all mine. He was violent, crazy, and high . . .
a condition known as The Municipal Court Triple
Crown.

The police arrested him on his way to my
courtroom, with his loaded gun tucked under his
coat. This, of course, along with his wife's com-
plaint, generated a new set of charges that were
assigned to another judge for hearing. At
sentencing, that judge administered the maximum
penalty and admonished: "I hope you'll think twice
before you threaten to kill that bitch again." I
suppose, in our own awkward way, that we do take
care of our own.

Chapter XIII
PEER POWER

In our criminal justice system, everyone has an absolute right to a jury trial if charged with an offense that might result in incarceration. In each case, the defendant and his/her attorney must decide whether a jury is necessary, or whether they will simply entrust their case to a judge. A jury trial is far more costly and time consuming than a simple trial to the bench, but for a defense attorney, the primary consideration is the attitude of the judge. If the judge is likely to find your client guilty and impose a stiff sentence, then your only hope is a jury. On the other hand, if the facts of the case are particularly offensive, a client may be far better off with a judge. Child abuse, cruelty to animals, abuse of the elderly or the mentally ill are far better suited for a bench trial. Jurors are visitors in the slippery world of crime. The judge lives there, and is less likely to be shocked by gruesome facts.

There are, of course, other reasons to prefer a jury. High profile cases involving substantial community controversy and publicity are generally best disposed of in front of a jury. This certainly takes the judge off the proverbial political hot seat.

Most jury trials occur because there is no doubt that the judge, sitting alone, would convict the accused. A perfect example is the typical drunk driving trial. Most of these trials involve repeat offenders whose customary defense is that they only had two beers and were weaving all over the road in order to avoid a puppy that ran into the path of their automobile. Now, most jurors drink — most jurors drink moderately and drive — so there is a built–in *there–but– for–the–grace–of–God* factor. Juries are not permitted access to the accused's prior criminal record, and they tend to believe people under oath must be telling the truth. It's something of an American tradition.

Thus, the jurors are never told that this is the accused's fifth encounter with a puppy. When the accused was asked to perform the finger–to–nose test he, without ceremony, placed his index finger in his ear. The jury is told that this occurred because he was so disoriented by his nearly catastrophic encounter with the puppy that he was unable to concentrate on the police officer's instructions. The accused was unable to walk a straight line because earlier in the evening, while clog–dancing with the lovely Wanda Louise at the bar, he broke off the heel of his boot, thus accounting for his general appearance of instability.

The defendant's friends all testify that he drank only two beers during his six hours at the bar. The defendant's blood alcohol content was three times the legal limit, the jury is told, because the police officer was simply "out to get" the defendant, and lied about the test result. The officer turned mean after the defendant threatened him, calling him every conceivable derogatory name. This, the jury is told, occurred because nobody should have to put up with such unjust accusations and unreasonable restraint of liberty. After all, this is a free country.

Frankly, I don't know any judge who would be inclined to acquit the defendant on these facts. But I have seen juries, time and time again, vote to find the defendant not guilty, thus preserving the American way. Nowhere in the law is the presumption of innocence so strong as in a drunk driving case.

Juries have an unpredictable, mystical quality. Judges, on the contrary, tend to be enormously predictable. The new–age defense lawyer hires a jury "expert" to assist in the selection of the most biased and defense–minded panel available. This is basic courtroom taxidermy. The prosecution rarely, if ever, engages in this practice because most jurors are pre–biased in favor of law and order — their personalities molded through the fear and guilt that helps a society based on laws function.

These jury "experts" are supposed to determine, through questioning and body– language diagnosis, which prospective jurors would vote for the underdog, regardless of the quality or veracity of the testimony. For example, a prospective juror who sits with crossed arms and legs during questioning is not an "open" person. The arm–crossers tend to be methodical, factual, conservative, literal, and defensive. The defense expert generally prefers a juror who is relaxed, open–legged, and slouched. This is an "open" person –– spiritual, non–judgmental, liberal, ethereal, and indecisive. Indecision is key. All criminal juries must be unanimous in their verdicts, so it takes only one loose cannon to create a hung jury.

Every now and then we meet a prospective juror who defies diagnosis — a true ringer. Jurors in our county are selected from a pool of registered voters. Prospective jurors are summoned to the courthouse and sequestered until they are called for duty. The bailiff is dispatched to retrieve a panel of about twenty people for selection. It is the bailiff's job to carefully line up the jurors before they enter the courtroom, because everyone is assigned a seat by name and number. The first eight jurors, the primary jury, are seated in the jury box. Those remaining are assigned seats, by number, in the first two rows of general seating. There is a rhythm and a ritual in this process reminiscent of a traditional Catholic wedding ceremony.

The attorneys are given a biographical sketch of each prospective juror. Each attorney questions the jurors and each may excuse three jurors without stating any reason. As a juror is excused, he or she is replaced from the general pool, seated in the front of the courtroom. Additional jurors may be excused *for cause*, generally when a juror expresses a substantial bias in the case, or indicates that he/she would be unable to follow the law as a matter of conscience. For example, one juror was asked if he had ever been the victim of a crime. He answered that he had been robbed by the defendant in the case at hand. Not only was he promptly excused, but the entire panel was excused because the process was, as we say in the law, tainted.

Some challenges for cause are a bit more complicated. On one occasion, I entered the courtroom to find a strikingly disheveled man seated in the alternate panel. He wore a red beanie with a yellow propeller whirling on top of his head. Clearly, he did not belong, or — yes, I admit it — I hoped he didn't belong.

My courtroom was located directly across the hall from the public rest rooms. A long, narrow bench stretched down the hall on either side of my courtroom door. This bench had, at one time or another, been the resting place for every wino in the city. In the morning the rest rooms were used to freshen up for a full day of drinking and street living. It was my own mini skid–row. Periodically, one of the winos overdid his morning toilette and water overflowed from the restroom into the hall, and, ultimately, onto the carpet in my courtroom. The water would creep toward the bench while attorneys sloshed around, unplugging the electrical appliances. I had become familiar with the regulars and we would exchange pleasantries every morning as I made my way through the smoke, pop cans, cigarette butts, empty potato chip bags, and assorted bodily fluids that adorned the approach to my courtroom. It was obvious to me that Mr. Beanie had slipped past the bailiff into the jury line as they waited in the hall to enter the courtroom.

As the attorneys began questioning the prospective jurors, I handed the bailiff a note: "GET HIM OUT OF HERE." The bailiff returned the note to me with the simple written reply: "I CAN'T." At that point, I politely interrupted the prosecutor and had a side–bar conference with the bailiff. "What do you mean you can't?" I began. "Are you too busy? I mean it. Get him out of here!" He replied, "I can't. He's on the jury." Well, for a moment, I was convinced that I was on "Candid Court TV." I summoned the attorneys to the bench to discuss this most delicate legal dilemma. They too thought that Mr. Beanie was a skid–row escapee, a regular who manned the hallway bench as often as I was on the courtroom bench. We hurriedly discussed our options. Either side could excuse Mr. Beanie without giving any reason. But neither attorney wanted to squander their challenges.

There is absolutely no legal precedent which would allow a judge to excuse a juror simply because he looks funny. I took a brief recess to assess the situation. As the jury exited the room, Mr. Beanie pushed his way through the throng, ran directly across the hall, and disappeared into the restroom clearly marked WOMEN. That was it. We all agreed, with relief, that he could be excused for cause.

Jury selection can be very exhausting for prospective jurors, who are prisoners in the Commissioner's office until they are summoned by a judge. To help the hours pass, jurors often have the foresight to bring their books, papers, knitting, and radios. One juror came to my courtroom with her small, hand–held radio. She appeared somewhat distracted, but otherwise normal in appearance and demeanor. As the attorneys questioned the other jurors, she would hold the radio to her ear, slowly moving her head to the music. I watched for about five minutes, then handed the bailiff a note asking him to politely tell her he would hold the radio for her until after the trial. She complied and he took the radio into my chambers.

She made the cut, chosen to sit on that jury, on a case that lasted for two days. After the verdict was returned, the juror came to my chambers to retrieve her radio. I heard the bailiff ask her why it had no batteries. She answered, "I never use them."

Despite everyone's best efforts, sometimes a jury of your peers isn't all it's cracked up to be.

Chapter XIV
SOUND JUDGMENT

Psychology tells us that the average person retains somewhat less than fifty percent of what he or she hears. The human mind simply was not meant to remain fixed upon the spoken word. This is precisely why judges must be paid. It is totally unreasonable to expect a person to voluntarily listen to total strangers for five hours a day without significant compensation. The courtroom is almost exclusively verbal. Excepting the occasional gory exhibit, there is no relief from the spoken word.

Picture, if you will, Oprah Winfrey after five hours of continuous talk show hosting. She gained all that weight back and she's only on the air for one hour perday. Besides that, she talks a lot of the time, so it would actually take ten hours of Oprah to equal five hours of court time. The way I figure it, if Oprah were a judge, she'd weigh about four hundred pounds by now, just from the stress of listening, listening, listening. Perhaps the closest thing to being a judge is being a psychiatrist, but even they limit their listening to one person in one hour segments. They appreciate the limits of the human mind.

In high–volume courts the regular morning docket consists of miscellaneous motions, one or two jury trials, and approximately twenty–five cases which are all set for trial. This brings with it at least two prosecutors, ten attorneys, and about forty witnesses, including several police officers. Everyone wants his or her case called first. At 9:00 a.m., the room is abuzz with the happy sound of plea bargaining, and the unhappy sound of threats of more serious prosecution.

Plea bargaining is that process whereby a defendant enters a plea of guilty to one charge in exchange for the dismissal of another charge, or the lessening of the original charge. It is a necessary evil in a metropolitan court system. If everyone entitled to a jury trial actually went to trial, the court system would collapse. It is absolutely impossible to dispose of the high volume of cases without plea bargaining.

Consequently, the typical day begins with a roll–call of those who have perfected a plea bargain. These cases are disposed of rather briskly and either a sentence is issued on the spot, or the case is continued for a more in–depth analysis of the defendant's criminal background. Further investigation often requires a psychiatric evaluation. By 11:00 a.m., the court is ready to begin hearing cases which could not be resolved by plea bargaining.

Around 2:00 p.m. — or twenty witnesses — (whichever comes first), the powers of concentration tend to lapse. It is important to devise exercises to pump oxygen back into the brain. The "full–mouth–open" yawn is discouraged, but the under–the–bench stretch is effective and invisible. This should be immediately followed by chanting the mantra, *There is life outside this courtroom. . .* over and over and over.

Around 3:00 p.m. is my personal worst, particularly if there has been no break for lunch. This is prime time for the "delirium daydream." On one such occasion, the prosecutor was examining the victim of an assault (verbally — a physical examination would probably have kept all of us more alert). The assault had occurred late at night, in a bar. Both participants were women, and both were, predictably, intoxicated. The only other thing they had in common was their man. It was a story as old as alcohol itself, a story repeated in the lyrics of tacky songs as long as there's been country music.

The victim was indescribably homely, and my attention lagged as she droned on about events leading up to her unfortunate encounter with the bar room floor. The last thing I remember was her saying she had been hit in the face, then thrown to the floor and kicked. The next thing I knew, a pair of large dentures slid across my bench like a hockey puck, struck the far side of the bench and bounced back to rest directly in front of me. Clearly, unlike those of us who were employees of the court, the victim had had a lunch break, and her lunch had included, but was not limited to, green leafy vegetables. Yuck! The cracked denture showed other signs of violence. Not only was this an improper way to enter evidence into the record, but it forced the victim to continue her testimony toothless.

Ordinarily, the defense attorney examines the evidence carefully, then it is marked as an exhibit by the court reporter. In this case, the defense lawyer simply stated: "I have no objection to that exhibit." What he should have said was "Gotcha!" The court reporter approached the bench, took one look at the exhibit, and said: "I'm not touching that until you put it in a plastic bag." God had blessed me on that day. There was no jury, so my embarrassment was confined to the trial participants. I wondered what damn fool had let this happen? But I knew there was no point in talking to yourself.

These mini–strokes, or lapses in full attention, are quite another matter when they occur in front of a jury. I recall snapping–to one day when I heard a witness say, "Sorry, I didn't wear my good panty hose today." I don't know how it happened. I plead exhaustion. But as I looked up at the witness, she had pulled her skirt up to her shoulders, exposing her panty hose and everything inside them, directly in front of the jury. The witness, a security guard at a large local department store, was fairly inexperienced in the courtroom, but not as inexperienced as the prosecutor who had asked her to demonstrate the concept of the *booster girdle*. This garment is an extra–large girdle with a pregnancy–type pouch, used by professional shop–lifters. The defendant was charged with theft. The prosecution alleged that she took three dresses from a display rack to the dressing room, and stuffed them into the booster girdle. On the sidewalk outside the store, she was arrested. This is a potentially dicey moment, because if an innocent person is confronted, he/she will almost certainly sue for false arrest. You can't stop and arrest women for being fat or pregnant. That would really be un–American.

In this case, however, the security guard had seen the defendant enter the store and she was convinced that a pregnancy was unlikely to come to term in the dressing room. She had a good case and a conviction was entered by the jury in record time. Apparently, her panty hose display was helpful in their deliberations, but I couldn't help wondering what makes otherwise reasonable people do such strange things simply because they are in a courtroom. After my years in a courtroom, I also can't help wondering if I'd find it easier to stay awake in the more stimulating environment of store detective work? Nah, I don't have the panty hose for that line of work. Now there's another reason for liking that black robe.

Chapter XV
THE MASCOT OF BEDLAM

Every justice system has its regulars, the people who, through happenstance or bizarre design, are constantly embroiled in the legal process. The Princess Fifi– Running Water– Taft– Nixon– Kennedy– Rockefeller is my personal favorite. She is affectionately known as 'The Feef.'

In her younger years, the Feef visited the courthouse every Monday, Wednesday, Friday, and Saturday. Weekdays, she would walk down the hallway and fling open the main door to each courtroom, yelling "How ya doin', Sexy?" to her favorite judges. Sometimes, she would sashay into a courtroom and take a seat in the witness stand, carefully raising her right hand to imitate the swearing–in process. She would testify with commitment and emotion for about a minute, then exit the courtroom as quickly as she had entered. What she said made absolutely no sense, but you could tell she was sincere. I think she had a notion that she could testify herself to morning regularity.

After completing her early rounds, the Feef would make her way to the Clerk's Office, where she would file some documents she claimed were lawsuits. The Feef has filed hundreds of lawsuits. She has sued Presidents, Kings, and Congress persons and, according to her, she has won them all. All of her written communications were drafted in a circle on the page, often with the lines illegibly overlapping. This technique was acquired, the Feef said, while she was enrolled at Harvard, Vassar, and Northwestern. In any case, this skill was perfected just before her torrid affair with Elvis Presley.

Following her visit to the Clerk's Office, she would stop in the public rest room to "powder her nose." Once inside, the Feef customarily used the very first stall on the right. It was, after all, hers. It was hers because she had written HERS on the front of the door with magic marker. Everyone who worked in the Courthouse knew it was HERS, but every now and then, a member of the public would mistakenly enter the Feef's private stall, mistaking it for just another public toilet. Feef had developed a system to discourage such activity and she delighted in surprising the unsuspecting interloper.

The Feef would quietly enter the adjoining stall and, at the appropriate moment, she would rasp, "Pssst, hey! You pee just like my dead sister!" The Feef does not now have, nor has she ever had a sister, but that line clears her personal stall in a matter of seconds. Let's face it; it's a tough line to answer. I once heard someone respond, "Thank you." Another polite soul answered piously, "I'm sorry for your loss." I knew how they felt. There just isn't a good response to such a remark.

I first met the Feef on a Saturday, about fifteen years ago when I was an inexperienced prosecutor, and the Feef was just as she is today. Saturdays were very special for the Feef. Every Saturday morning she attended court to post bail for the drunks locked up Friday night. They would follow her, single file, to her home, where they'd sign a power of attorney allowing her to receive and cash their government benefit checks. They became totally dependent upon the Feef for money and shelter and they would follow her around like puppy dogs. The Feef genuinely meant well, like a scruffy Peter Pan; everything she did was for the good of her lost boys.

This weekly ritual ended abruptly in the late 1970s, when the city opened a group of homeless shelters and drop-in centers. The police would deliver the drunks to these designated shelters, rather than to the already overcrowded jail. The Feef's business was rapidly drying up. At one point, the Feef, out of desperation, signed up for the free government cheese and butter give-away. She stood in line each day, returning to her apartment with a pound of cheese and a pound of butter. The program ended in late March, but the Feef's butter trouble didn't begin until summer.

By August, approximately twenty pounds of butter had melted and dripped through the floor onto the tenants below. The Feef became agitated upon learning of her landlord's plan to evict her. She packed up her boys and a few articles of clothing, torching the building on her way out. Mercifully, no one was hurt and the building was not destroyed. The Feef, however, was charged with arson.

The charge later was reduced to criminal damaging, to which the Feef pled guilty. She defended her behavior by telling the judge that her despicable slum landlord never cleaned or fixed anything, so she was sure he would re-rent the flat without cleaning up her butter. This would, of course, attract rats, and she hated to do that to her long-time neighbors. So, the martyred Feef reasoned, the only way to save the neighborhood was to burn down the building.

The court personnel, as was their habit, took up a collection to set the Feef up in a different tenement. For her punishment, she had to agree to stay away from her former landlord, and stay off any property he owned. This was hardly what any prosecutor would call a slam–dunk victory, but I was delighted. The Feef had walked on this one, but, as a prosecutor, I felt that she then owed me one. Knowing the Feef's flair for the original, I thought this debt might come in handy.

Some months after the Feef's eviction, I was prosecuting a case in which two rival gangs had beaten each other senseless. These are tough cases to prosecute because both sides are probably lying. The defendants were so smart, so clever, so astute, that they decided to represent themselves. There were no independent witnesses and there was no way to determine who started the fight. This, of course, was the sole issue. As the trial dribbled on, the courtroom began to look like a wedding run amok. One gang sat on the right side of the courtroom glaring at the opposing gang, seated, of course, on the opposite side. There were no good guys; everyone in the room was a loser.

On a recess from this futile case, I saw the Feef wandering down the hall. The Feef was someone the Fashion Police would shoot on sight, and on this day, she wore a mini–skirt over a pair of men's cut–off pants and three or four shirts of different colors and patterns topped off the ensemble. Queen of the layered look, Fifi was also a designer. Once, she was arrested in the public library for taking a scissors to the coat of an unsuspecting and uncooperative library patron. She simply decided that his coat would be more fashionable vented on the side, instead of the traditional back vent. But back to the gang trial and my unexpected encounter with the Feef. As luck would have it, the gang fight had occurred but two blocks from the Feef's new apartment. Bingo! I would call her as a witness, even though it was not clear if the Feef knew anything about the case. I, the clever prosecutor, would bring in an "independent" witness and the defendants would fold, confessing to starting the fight. They knew the judge would convict them if it became anything more than a liars' match. Yep, this would tip the scales of justice and the taxpayers would be well–served.

The Feef was a perfect witness, a prosecutor's dream. She stated her name and address clearly on request. Asked if she was aware of the fight, she replied lucidly in the affirmative. Then, without missing a breath, she added that John F. Kennedy fathered her six children, and that she was running for Governor of Kentucky in the next general election. I asked her to wait in the hall until she was needed to testify later in the trial. You would never want the Feef confined in a closed room for long because she was chronically hygienically–challenged.

As the Feef left the courtroom, I glanced at the judge, who was holding his hand over his mouth. The defendants couldn't see his smile, but they did see his eyes roll, and sensed that something very important had just occurred. He was grinning because he, too, admired the Feef, and he thought I had done this for comic relief during this otherwise stultifying trial. While I am not now and was not then above such pranks, this time I had a serious plan.

The gang–leader was the first to testify for the defense. He was a burly, scraggly young man with that pasty, opaque, lived–all–his–life–under–a–rock look. He was living proof that Darwin was very, very wrong. He was also living proof that nonlinear, self–sustaining genealogy and intra–familial marriages over several generations are not a good thing. His eyes were so close together that God had to place the bridge of his nose at an abnormally low level, almost directly above his upper lip. He was the perfect demonstration case for those who believe that, outside the British Royal Family, cousins shouldn't marry.

On the witness stand, he presented the classic W.T.D.K.N. (pronounced Whit–Kin) defense. . .

Wasn't There; Don't Know Nothing. When he finished testifying, I asked him what he would say if I told him that my independent witness, Ms. Rockefeller, saw him start the fight. He replied, indignantly, with his tatoos quivering righteously: "She'd be lyin' 'cause I didn't start that fight. All I did was tell my buddies to start the fight. Then I got into it to help them." He not only shot himself in the foot, he managed to blow all of his buddies away with the same shot. Now, here was a double–damn fool. First he represented himself; then, he let the Feef unravel his defense. The Feef had saved the day. Now we were even.

The Feef and I have grown older together. I'm now in my forties, and she is in her Metamucil years, and we're both as crazy as ever. Most of her boys have died, including her very special beau, Baldy. Everyone could see that Baldy was special to her, because he was chosen to walk directly behind the Feef in the Pied–Piper parades. There was even talk of a marriage, but Baldy's liver "ate him up," as the Feef explained, before the nuptials could be arranged.

Despite her personal tragedies, the Feef remains a lady with a mission. She is there for the underdog. She still attends every major trial in the courthouse. She carries her placards and banners — FREE PETE ROSE, HANG MARVIN

WARNER — but, all in all, she is a pretty good barometer of public opinion. I hope she outlasts us all.

Chapter XVI
THE LORD WILLING

Freedom of religion is one of our most precious constitutional rights, and courts are loath to interfere with the practice and exercise of religious beliefs. This is because spiritual reality is such a special, fragile, and relative concept. We recognize, in the law, that each person must come to his/her own conclusions about the Almighty. It is only when one's spiritual practices run afoul of man's laws that the courts are called upon to intervene.

The case of Arvil the Sign Man was one such conflict. Arvil was a fairly typical street person except that he was sent to earth to save evil men from their evil ways. To this end, Arvil would get up every morning and, just as if he were reporting for a job, walk to the county jail and parade in front of it with a large homemade sign that said **REPENT**. Arvil would hold the sign toward heaven so inmates high up in the jail could see it from their tiny windows. Some inmates would wave at Arvil; some would shake their fists; and others would yell at him. Arvil was part of the scenery — a surrealistic part — but a part, nonetheless.

Arvil began his daily picket at seven each morning and he concluded directly after his coffee break, four hours later. He was there in the rain, in the snow, and during bright, cloudless sunny days. Arvil was a regular. After he finished his faithful tour of duty at the jail, he would walk to the downtown shopping area, where he spent the afternoon trying to sell homemade Holy Cross necklaces. Each necklace was made of white yarn, which Arvil glued to a piece of cross–shaped cardboard.

On his walk to town one day, Arvil was accosted by a group of teen–age boys who began to taunt him. Arvil responded by smacking them with his **REPENT** sign until the city police were summoned. Arvil was arrested and convicted of assault, sentenced to twenty days in jail, where he was to become a very popular fellow.

While incarcerated, Arvil began selling his cross necklaces to inmates scheduled to appear in court, advising them that their judge would certainly give them a break if they demonstrated they had found Jesus while awaiting trial. I had never seen so many defendants find Jesus as when Arvil was locked up. It was like a Christmas miracle.

The day after Arvil was released from jail, he was back into his routine with a brand new

REPENT sign, but now he marched at the entrance to the judge's parking lot. His stint in the slammer had shown him that the evil people were not in jail at all — they were on the bench.

Fanatic and delusional piety often can be cause for psychiatric concern. But distinguishing delusional religiosity from moderate or socially acceptable religiosity can be very problematic for the courts. The plea of "not guilty by reason of insanity" is very common in extreme cases. This is a very complicated legal defense, which is very often misunderstood by the public. Most legal scholars would agree, however, that the concept is really quite simple. When God talks directly to you, we all know that He tells you to do good things. So, if God tells you to do bad things, illegal things, dangerous things — then you aren't really talking to God at all — in which case you are crazy, and probably should be in an appropriate institution.

Sometimes it's not this simple. For example, in the very early days of the abortion protest movement, it was common to have a lone protester arrested for trespassing on the clinic property. If his reason was that God told him to do it, he generally was ordered to undergo psychiatric counseling. Today, however, thousands of people claim that God has spoken to them, ordering them to trespass on clinic property. Clearly, the more people God talks to, the less likely it is that a psychiatric evaluation will be ordered by the courts.

So, for the "not guilty by reason of insanity" plea to be effective, the following criteria must be met:

1. The defendant must be alone when God speaks to him/her;
2. God must tell him/her to do a very bad thing;
3. He/she must do the bad thing which, coincidentally, is illegal.

It's so simple, yet so complicated. It's just another metaphysical tightrope that must be traversed by the judge, to whom, unfortunately, God so rarely speaks directly.

Chapter XVII
NECTAR OF THE GODS

Nothing contributes more to the misery of the human condition than alcohol. There is also nothing which contributes so greatly to the perpetuation of the criminal justice system. I have been personally involved in creating treatment programs as alternatives to incarceration, but dockets continue to be clogged with cases involving alcohol.

The theory behind treatment programs is that alcoholics, or the alcoholically challenged, will return immediately to a life of crime after serving a sentence in jail. My experience indicates that this is true, as we see the same people in court over and over again, drunker and drunker.

The concept of treatment is that, first, the defendant must admit that there is a problem. Then, the treatment counselors concentrate on demonstrating how to exist without consuming massive quantities of alcohol. This traditional treatment program is successful in about fifty per cent of all cases. Jail, on the other hand, is successful only as long as the defendant remains a guest of the state. What is especially troubling is the fifty per cent failure rate of traditional treatment alternatives. These become the hopeless cases that circle through the justice system like a busy department store's revolving door.

No matter what is done, there are people who will continue to drink and commit crimes. Alcoholism is a social problem, but it becomes a legal problem when the offender is a mean drunk. It seems to me that what, or how much, people drink is not the court's business. Drinking is a problem for families, relationships, and employment, but is not, per se, a problem for the courts. The alcoholics in the fifty per cent failure group are those who simply can't be pleasant, happy, self–destructive drunks. They have to drive, fight, abuse, and destroy everything and everyone around them. So far, the treatment experts have not devised a reasonable alternative for these hopeless types who appear repeatedly in the courts.

After considerable thought and experience in working with chronic alcoholics, I have dreamed up a model treatment alternative, **MDS**, or The Mean Drunk School. MDS is similar to a rat maze with a variety of individual treatment rooms, all equipped with standard cattle prods.

Upon acceptance into the MDS — following strict admission requirements involving repeated drinking–related crimes in which others have been killed, hurt, threatened, etc., and failure in other treatment programs — the mean drunk would be given all the alcohol he or she requires, upon demand. Drinking heavily is encouraged by all MDS counselors. The Mean Drunk School would admit both men and women, to best assimilate the real world of mean drunks, since this area is one of the sorriest in which women have come a long way, baby.

During the first week of MDS training, the mean drunk would be placed in the Street Scene Room. This room contains plate glass store–fronts, and a faux bar entrance. The goal in this room is to arrive at the bar entrance without a single mean encounter. First, the mean drunk must stagger past a police officer walking the beat. Instead of approaching the officer with the customary threat of bodily harm, the mean drunk is trained to say, "Evening, Officer, how nice to see you again. How're the wife and kids?" Once this exercise is successfully completed, the mean drunk moves on to the prostitute on the street. He may do whatever he likes with the prostitute, so long as he treats her with respect and does not assault her. Phase One is completed when the mean drunk is able to pass all glass store fronts without bashing them in. These exercises are practiced until the mean drunk is successful.

After a brief graduation ceremony, where more alcohol is served, the mean drunk enters the Phase Two treatment room. This room is a typical bar interior, complete with pool table, jukebox, and mean, drunk women. Props include breakable bar stools and assorted weapons, including switch-blade knives, brass knuckles, and the increasingly popular Uzi. Here, with the assistance of the cattle prod, the mean drunk learns to be pleasant in the face of adversity. He is taught to tell truly funny jokes, and to say "No, thank you. I really don't want to fight you." He also learns not to throw people or objects.

Phase Three is a parking lot. Here, the mean drunk is given a significant temptation. The parking lot contains one Corvette, one Cadillac, and one fully–loaded conversion van, all brand new, unlocked, with keys in their ignitions. The van contains a wet bar, snacks, a TV set, a telephone, and a couple of scantily–clothed, mean, drunk women in white plastic go–go boots. Counselors direct the mean drunk to the van for a drink. Then, the mean drunk is released into the parking lot, without supervision. Each ignition key is wired directly into a standard 220 volt outlet, and each vehicle is specially equipped with a driver's side ejection seat. This is the mean drunk's designated driver exercise. Once the mean drunk learns that he must always ride in the passenger seat, he is moved to Phase Four.

The next and in some ways most challenging treatment area, Phase Four, is the Family Room. Upon successful completion of the bar scene and the parking lot situation, the mean drunk returns to his faux home. He is taught to always stagger into the house without breaking anything, starting by entering with a key, breaking the old habit of kicking in the door. The family room contains six screaming children and one mean, angry wife. She immediately confronts the mean drunk with the usual litany: "You useless drunk; I can't stand the sight of you!" Now, the mean drunk is taught not to beat or otherwise molest the little woman or anyone else in the home. Instead, he is taught that he must say "Goodnight, Honey, see you in the morning." Due to alcoholic dementia, these short phrases are often difficult for the mean drunk to remember. Thus, the mean drunk is taught to use prepared flash cards containing appropriate, non-violent phrases. The famous Miranda warnings are printed on the reverse side of the flash cards, just in case anything goes wrong.

Following graduation from Phase Four, the mean drunk is placed in a half-way house full of other mean drunks. Following the Alcoholics Anonymous model, each mean drunk is assigned to a buddy. The buddies are joined together at the wrists, with traditional handcuffs. They are given all the alcohol they want, then released. This is a very difficult real–world assignment.

As in traditional treatment programs, relapses are to be expected. The buddy system is extremely beneficial in this event, because the mean drunks probably will simply fight each other, without involving total strangers or the police. Already hand–cuffed, the mean drunks are easier to arrest, and the risk of escape is minimal.

Upon the successful completion of the MDS half–way house experience, the mean drunk attends a gala graduation celebration and is returned to his real streets, his real bars, and his home. But he is not returned to the courts, and that would be a true success story.

Yeah, the MDS is just a judge's daydream, just a way to avoid the despair that follows any attempt to deal with the overwhelming problems of alcohol related crime. It just isn't funny.

Chapter XVIII
PICKING THE ODDS

Sometimes very good things happen to very bad people. That strange bounce of the judicial hole every now and then allows a happy ending, but the odds are about the same as successfully challenging a speeding ticket in court. Now, to beat a speeding ticket, either the police officer has retired to Florida or he is deceased. Since younger officers tend to be assigned to radar details, your chances are approximately the same as the chance of winning the lottery.

Clyde–John was one such winner in the judicial lottery. Clearly, his name was backwards. It should have been John–Clyde, but his mother knew he was different and, to her, very special. Clyde–John specialized in petty theft, street robbery, and fencing hot merchandise. He was particularly fond of the elderly and the infirm. Through it all, his Mama was supportive and helpful. Every time Clyde–John was accused of a crime, she appeared on his behalf as an alibi witness. She was not noticeably intelligent or creative, so the alibi was always the same: "Judge, Clyde–John is the victim of police harassment. He couldn't have robbed nobody. He was home with me that night and we was watching the champeen wreslin' on the TV." She always used this alibi because it worked once, and a jury acquitted Clyde–John. She knew better than to mess with a good thing.

One summer evening, Clyde–John was leaning against the tenement wall on his corner. This was how he established his territory, a ritual much like that one that has worked for dogs for centuries. It was a shoddy corner, surrounded by bars and pawn shops, and one small grocery store existing to sell wine and lottery tickets. It was here that Clyde–John met Tyrone Williams. Tyrone's nickname was "The Fly."

The Fly, injured in an industrial accident in the early sixties, was a wheelchair–bound double amputee. He was blessed with a great sense of humor and cursed with an addiction to alcohol and pain medication. But mostly, the Fly was a survivor. He knew what had to be done to make it on the streets. The first time I met the Fly was in the summer of 1975, when he was charged with discharging a firearm while intoxicated and inciting a riot.

The facts were uncontroverted. The Fly was on his way to his favorite bar when he was confronted by a group of four adolescent thugs. They wanted his money; they wanted his watch; and, they were in a hurry. Their girlfriends were up the street watching as they approached the slow–moving Fly. "Give us everything you got!" they demanded. The Fly did as instructed. He removed a revolver from under his lap blanket and shot into the air. "That's what I got, you Muthers. . . now get on the ground!" As the thugs dropped to the pavement, six patrons of the nearby bar came outside to see what was happening. The Fly told his friends about the attempted robbery, then scooted into the bar.

Their innate distrust for the police and the court system persuaded the Fly's friends to handle the matter themselves. They took turns kicking the boys as they lay face–down on the sidewalk. Realizing that the situation had gotten out of control, the girlfriends ran to call the police. When the officers arrived, all they could see was a street brawl in which the young boys were clearly the victims. The Fly was inside the bar having a drink to calm his nerves. The boys were transported to the hospital for treatment of various cuts and bruises, and all of the Fly's friends were charged with assault and hauled off to jail. Later that evening, the police unraveled the story and the Fly was arrested the next day, along with the four boys. Ultimately, everyone was convicted and everyone received a minimum sentence. Sometimes, street justice is the best rehabilitation possible.

Clyde–John didn't know the history of the Fly. It was too long ago and the neighborhood had changed. It had become far worse, controlled almost entirely by drug gangs and street prostitutes. The Fly had changed too; he was seventy–two years old and partially blind. Most of his friends were dead or dying, and the younger men in the bar didn't seem enraptured by his memories of the neighborhood.

Clyde–John watched as the Fly slowly made his way to the local grocery store. To Clyde–John, the Fly was the perfect victim: he couldn't chase anyone and he must have money, because he'd just gone to the store. The Fly, as always, had a tattered blanket on his lap to shield what remained of his legs. He placed a small sack of groceries on the blanket and slowly proceeded back onto the street. Clyde–John approached from the rear and shoved the Fly's wheelchair toward the alley. The Fly struggled to turn around. His groceries fell to the ground as he was whisked around the corner. Of course, Clyde–John always carried a gun, but he didn't bother to pull it out for this job. It was all too quick, too simple to require a weapon.

Clyde–John came around to the front of the wheelchair and confronted the Fly, face to face. "Give me your money, old man; I don't wanta hurt you." The Fly yelled, "I don't wanta hurt you either!" as he pulled his revolver from beneath the blanket and fired a shot directly over Clyde–John's head. The Fly didn't want to kill anyone, but he didn't want to be messed over either. As he pulled the gun out, a pint of wine fell from the wheelchair, shattering when it hit the concrete. This time the Fly hoped the police would come; this time he knew there weren't any friends to run to his rescue. But Clyde–John ran as fast and as far as he could, because he knew the police would be coming. Someone would have heard the gun shot. He ran into a second alley and stripped off his shirt, to confuse the Fly.

As the bare–chested Clyde–John was catching his breath, three teenage boys entered the alley. They were all running and one of them was carrying a purse. Clyde–John knew that they had just robbed a women. So that the day wouldn't be a total loss, Clyde–John pulled his gun from his pants, jumped into the center of the alley, and said: "Hold it! Give me that purse." At that very moment, two police officers came running into the alley with their guns drawn. Clyde–John had become an instant hero. In five minutes he had gone from criminal to star witness. The owner of the purse was an elderly lady who, like the Fly, had just left the corner grocery. She was very grateful to Clyde–John and rewarded him with $20 for capturing the young thieves.

Clyde–John's mother was very proud, but had always known he was a good boy. Community leaders praised his bravery and he was about to receive the neighborhood's Crimefighter's Award. However, his celebrity did not go unnoticed by the elderly Fly. Two days after the purse incident, the true story came to the attention of the police. The Fly reported the attempted robbery and accused Clyde–John. The police went to the alley and found a bullet hole in the side of the building where the Fly said he shot over his assailant's head. They also found the broken pint bottle of wine.

Not surprisingly, Clyde–John's mother refused to believe the Fly, but the police did. And so did the Grand Jury. But what are the odds that a common street robber will select a drunk, gun–wielding, partially blind, seventy–two year old double amputee as his perfect victim? It's probably about the same as beating a speeding ticket. But for that one brief, shining moment, Clyde–John had won the judicial lottery, and to his mother he would always be a hero. Maybe it's all in a name after all.

Chapter XIX
THE DUCKS THAT WEREN'T

In law, as in life, things rarely are as they appear. I have always had a keen desire to know and understand how and why things happen. It is that basic "What is the nature of the universe?" mentality. It is the same quality found in the nosy neighbor or the everyday office busy–body. It is that personality type which is driven to observe life and attempt to explain it, rather than just live it.

I think, for good or evil, that most judges demonstrate this personality characteristic. One very senior judge advised me that his success on the bench was due to his refusal to talk in the courtroom except when absolutely necessary. In his view, it was a mistake to ever comment on a case in the courtroom. This was because anything you said could be cause for appeal, or worse, it would become obvious through your comments that you didn't know anything about the case that you had just heard. His theory was simple. Let the attorneys talk, nod appropriately, and issue your finding. But never, never ask **WHY**. I believe that this judge is the exception, but I also believe that he is one of the dullest human beings I have ever met. I have always used his advice, however, as a sign of total burn–out. What is most interesting in the routine of trial work, to me, is the **WHY** of all behavior. How can I sit through trials and not ask questions like "Why did you steal a city bus?" or "Why did you sign you mother's name to a stolen check?" or "Why have you appeared in my courtroom seventeen times in the last three years?" It seems to me that when that question, **WHY,** becomes unimportant, it's time to fold up your torts and retire.

I have discovered that it is almost always a mistake to simplify and categorize criminal behavior. I heard a case recently in which a young man entered a plea of guilty to the theft of a Metro bus. The defendant was eighteen years old, had no prior criminal record, and to all appearances, was an average teenager. I was particularly tickled by the case, because I have always wanted to drive one of those hogs myself.

In this case, the bus driver had left the idling bus unattended, and gone across the street to a phone booth. It was the last stop on the route and the bus was empty. The driver watched through the dirty glass of the phone booth as the defendant entered the bus, sat down in the driver's seat, then drove away. The driver ran into the street in time to see the bus come to rest smack in the middle of a group of parked cars. The defendant was not seriously injured, but the cars were terminal.

In court, the defendant appeared remorseful as his attorney told me it was a stupid teenage prank that had gone terribly wrong. The defendant never spoke. This is not unusual, because most attorneys instruct their clients not to talk in court. Too many defendants have a tendency to take a bad situation and turn it into a total disaster.

Now, this was a perfect **WHY?** kind of a case. Stealing a bus for fun was something I could understand. But what didn't make sense to me was that the defendant was all alone when this incident occurred. He was not surrounded by a group of cheering friends. He was not showing off for his high school honey. He had not suffered any recent mental breakdown related to parental abuse, family break–up, etc. He was not a fraternity member. Nothing fit, nothing.

Prior to issuing a sentence, I ordered the probation department to interview the defendant and file a pre–sentence report. The **WHY?** of the case was soon revealed. The defendant was severely retarded. He was functioning at the level of a five year old. For weeks he had heard the catchy little jingle on the radio urging all to *"Ride*

share . . . take the bus, take the bus, take the bus."
And so, he did.

It is, perhaps, a universal experience to be caught in the web of guilty circumstance and appearance. I recall being interrupted by my beeper as I worked in my garden one late June evening. Judges are "on call" nights and weekends for the ever–popular midnight search warrants and bond settings.

On this night, the undercover narcotics unit needed a search warrant, and they had an informant who had to be interviewed by a judge. Informants are generally hard–core, career criminals with absolutely no regard for the traditional values of friendship. The first rule of search warrants is: Never let the police bring the informant to your house. For one thing, you have probably convicted the informant on numerous occasions and you certainly don't relish the thought of him knowing where you live. Second, I have never met an informant who did not also specialize in burglary to support his drug habit. So this is the last person you want sitting across from you at your kitchen table, taking note of every piece of property on the premises.

When I returned the telephone call on my beeper that June evening, I was pleased to learn that the police had their informant blindfolded in the back seat of an old junker car they affectionately call the sleazemobile. This group of agents pride themselves on appearing to be the dirtiest, hairiest, most disgusting thugs on the face of the earth. They made Hell's Angels look like a college fraternity. I arranged to meet this group at my usual spot . . . on the corner, at the mailbox, three blocks from my house. When it comes to drug busts, these guys are always in a hurry, so I left my house right after hanging up the phone, walking quickly to the corner rendezvous. We arrived at precisely the same time and an agent hopped out of the car and opened the back door for me. I was seated next to the blindfolded informant, as we sped to a nearby park for the interview. The warrant was issued and I was returned to my mailbox corner.

As I walked back toward my house, I saw three city police cars in my driveway. One police officer was on the front porch talking to my elderly neighbor. Another officer began yelling as he approached me, "Where the hell have you been?" As it turned out, my neighbor had been walking her equally elderly dog and had seen the mailbox meeting. She called the police to report that I had been kidnapped by thugs, one of whom had a gun. She could tell that it was a kidnapping, she explained, because one person was already blindfolded in the back of the car. Besides, she had known me for years, and I certainly wasn't the kind of person who stood on the corner and hitched rides with sleazy no–goods. It made perfect sense — but she never asked **WHY?** After all, if it looks like a duck, walks like a duck, quacks like a duck . . . it's a duck. Maybe.

Chapter XX
THE HAZARD OF OCCUPATION

Even the worst career criminals have some good in them, some redeeming quality. At least, that's what defense attorneys would have us believe. Before the judge imposes sentence, every defendant has the right to be heard. This is when the mitigation speech is presented to the judge. Attorneys don't make their clients; clients come "as is" with no warranties, and some without common sense or decency. The mitigation presentation often requires enormous creativity and ingenuity. As television struggles to fill sixty or more channels with programming, they're overlooking a good source of creativity — defense lawyers.

In my years as a judge, I have kept an unofficial tally of mitigation speeches. Most criminals are unemployed and unemployable. That unique combination of a total lack of skill and a total lack of motivation most often leads to a life of crime. The typical mitigation in such a case would be presented as follows:

"Judge, my client is remorseful. He is
twenty–four years old and the father of
three small children. He has been
supporting himself by doing odd jobs for
the last six years. He lives with his
aunt, Hilda–Jolene, an invalid in need
of constant care. He has a drug and
alcohol problem and is willing to enter
a treatment program. He was very
cooperative with the police during and
after his arrest."

Following the mitigation presentation, the
Judge carefully considers the facts of the case and
the defendant's past and present criminal record.
It becomes apparent after even the most cursory
review of the facts that the most truthful mitigation would have been:

"Judge, my client is remorseful because he
got caught. He has had quite a bit of
experience with crime and, frankly, he
thought he had learned from his past
exploits. Once again, he made a stupid
mistake. He is the father of three, all
of whom are being supported by the taxpayers
of this state. His odd jobs include odd
robbery, odd burglary, odd drug dealing, and

odd assault. His invalid aunt, Hilda–Jolene, has become increasingly displeased with him as a house guest. He doesn't clean up after himself; his low–life friends are all unemployed and into drugs; and she hasn't seen her Social Security checks since he moved in. He was cooperative with the police in that he turned informant in exchange for your consideration of a light sentence. So far, six of his close, personal friends have been arrested as a result."

As is often the case in the law, the omission is far more interesting than the commission.

My unofficial mitigation tally has also revealed that most employed defendants fall into four primary occupational categories:

(1) Drywall hangers/roofers

(2) Nursing home employees

(3) Hazardous waste or nuclear
     plant employees

(4) Food preparation employees

These occupations appear to be disproportionately represented. There is a strange causal relationship here that I am unable to explain or rationalize. I had a nightmare once in which I saw the entire city of Cincinnati surrounded by roofed dry wall. Inside the walled city there was a small nuclear explosion in which many people were injured. They were, of course, taken to nursing homes and forced to eat large quantities of chicken, hamburgers, pizza, and other fast food. I remain both hopeful and confident that this nightmare will never come to pass. Surely the late–stage alcoholic who handles hazardous waste or constructs nuclear plants is supervised by a sober, responsible adult. In any case, I have learned to hang my own dry wall, and I would rather die on the street than enter a nursing home. But, in my heart, I also know that my loving nephew, Narley, will commit me at the drop of my senile hat. There is simply nothing that can be done to prevent that unfortunate event.

This leaves only the food preparation worker. Every time an attorney mentions this occupation in mitigation, I ask the precise location and shift of the defendant's employment and restrict my dining accordingly. Having spent years as the "I fought anorexia and won" poster girl, I have a unique appreciation for food of all types. In fact, it has been suggested that upon by death, my tombstone should read: **NEVER MISSED A MEAL**. While I enjoy a Happy Meal as much as the next person, I know where those hands have been.

Chapter XXI
THE PERILS OF RODNEY

Experience tells us that human beings have an incredible propensity simply to be in the wrong place at the wrong time. To some degree, we have all experienced the dreadful folly of *spatial miscalculation*. It is a sick celestial joke. If being in the wrong place at the wrong time results in something good, then we call this propensity <u>fate</u>. Conversely, if something bad happens, we often call it a criminal conviction.

Rodney O'Conner was just such a spatially–challenged individual. Rodney was a slim, twenty–three year old construction worker. If it weren't for the limitations of his age, he would be a good–old–boy. He was a good–young–boy who just happened, at the whim of the universe, to be a magnet for misfortune. Rodney was blessed with a loving family, and he was especially fond of his sixteen year old niece, Megan. She was more like a little sister than a niece, and Rodney had even taught her how to drive a car.

Megan was a plump, happy–go–lucky, some–what below–average student at a local Catholic girl's school. Rodney often picked her up after school to get an afternoon snack before heading home. Rodney went to all of Megan's soccer games, and was a chaperon for her high school's dances. He was the perfect uncle.

Prior to obtaining her driver's license, Megan decided to borrow Uncle Rodney's pick–up truck for a little trip to a swimming party. This, of course, was without Rodney's permission or knowledge. When Rodney found out, he decided to teach Megan a lesson. What better way, he thought, than to embarrass Megan when he picked her up after school. To this end, Rodney took Megan's new pink prom dress and stowed it in his pick–up truck. After work, Rodney stopped his truck in front of the school and quickly slipped into the pink dress. He completed the outfit with a pair of sensible black pumps borrowed from his sister. The dress was just a touch too small, so Rodney was unable to zip the back zipper. He looked lovely, except for the strange sock marks on his legs and the tan marks on his upper arms, where his t–shirts usually covered him. Panty hose would have helped, but he had forgotten them. It was an omen of the misfortune that was to follow.

It was the wrong time for Rodney because the school children were all being released into the parking area. It was the wrong place for Rodney because there were three undercover police officers in the parking area, trying to catch a man seen masturbating in his car on several previous occasions. The officers watched carefully as Rodney struggled to remove his work clothes in the small cab of his truck. When he exited in the unzipped pink formal dress, the officers were convinced that they had their man. One plainclothes officer approached Rodney, grabbed his arm, and said: "You're coming with me, Sweetie." Rodney thought a pervert was trying to pick him up, so he shoved the officer away and ran toward the school to call the police. The two other undercover officers tackled Rodney and a struggle ensued. Although handcuffed, Rodney was relatively undamaged, but the pink dress was torn and soiled from the scuffle on the overheated spring asphalt. No one wanted to listen to Rodney's protests of innocence, and before it was all over, Rodney had been charged with public indecency, resisting arrest, and three counts of assault on a police officer.

Rodney wasn't drunk, he was not on drugs, and he had no criminal record. He was a freak in the criminal justice system. He was booked and released from the overcrowded jail after a delay because he didn't have a wallet, driver's license, or any other form of identification. All he had was the pink formal; the sensible black pumps had been lost in the scuffle. While Rodney was amusing the intake officers at the jail, his clothes and wallet were being liberated by a group of teenage entrepreneurs. This, of course, was before the police towed Rodney's truck from the school to the city's impoundment lot. It was there that Rodney suffered the ultimate indignity.

A barefoot and disheveled Uncle Rodney arrived at the impoundment lot. His unzipped, off–the–shoulder pink dress was bunched around his waist like a tu–tu and his chest was bare, except for a dangling gold cross. After the hysterical impoundment officers had finished with Rodney, he was reunited with his pick–up truck. The nightmare was almost over.

Understandably, Rodney was anxious to tell his version of the story. He wanted his day in court. As that day came to a close, I recall his attorney asking Rodney how he felt when the impoundment officers were mocking his attire. Rodney's response was shy and simple: "I felt cheap."

Rodney was, of course, found Not Guilty. But he had learned the cruel and retributive nature of *spatial miscalculation.* As far as I'm concerned, it should always be a felony to wear a pink off–the–shoulder prom dress with black pumps.

Chapter XXII
TACO SURPRISE

Those of us in the crime biz recognize the danger of recommending that citizens arm themselves and form neighborhood vigilante groups. More likely than not, innocent neighbors would become the victims of these groups. Not to mention pesky cats, dogs, and children who could be harmed by their hapless yet well–intentioned actions. But there are other ways of fighting crime, far more clever and exquisite ways of refusing to be victimized.

My personal nomination for the Crime Fighter of the Year award is Janie Simpson. When Janie became a crime fighter extraordinaire, she was an energetic thirty–five year old housewife. She was always on time, and she always paid her bills on the very day that they arrived in the mail. She obeyed the law and came no closer to a courtroom than the <u>Perry Mason</u> re-runs she watched while doing housework.

She never drove through (much less frequented) high crime areas, and she never went out alone at night. Her house was protected by both a large German shepherd and an expensive alarm system. Janie had never even known the victim of a crime, and the closest she ever came to a real live criminal was when she watched Geraldo. All this changed one day when Janie went to a suburban shopping center for lunch and a little shopping with some friends. Lunch was delicious and the shopping productive. As she returned to her car in the parking lot, laden with packages, she was confronted by Ray Williams, who escorted her, at gun point, to his nearby stolen car.

Ray was a large, menacing, and violent drug–addicted sort who had spent most of his twenty–eight years securely behind bars. He was a Parole Board success story, released early from his last incarceration because he was a model prisoner. It never seems to occur to the Parole Board that people are model prisoners because they are such experienced prisoners. If you've spent most of your life in prison, you ought to be good at it, and Ray was very, very good at it.

When Ray spotted Jane in that parking lot, it was love at first sight. He threw her into the driver's side of the car he'd stolen just minutes before, telling her to lie down on the seat or he would blow her head off. She began shaking uncontrollably, but in dreadful silence. She wanted to talk, to scream, to fight, but she couldn't; she was absolutely paralyzed with fear.

Within minutes, they were out of the shopping

center parking lot and onto an expressway. It was a full–blown kidnapping. Jane had taken a self–defense course at the YWCA and she knew that the best course of action was to catch the assailant off guard, but how? No one had practiced the speeding get–away car scenario with Janie. In fact, such a eventuality had never come up in the course.

Terrified of rape, frozen with fear, Janie did what came ever so naturally; she began to vomit. This was not lady–like, mouth–covered purging. Rather, it was Exorcist–type projectile vomiting, steaming, lump–laden vomit that covered the car's floor and windshield and, most importantly, Ray. He slammed Janie's head into the car seat and yelled that he would kill her if she didn't stop it. But she couldn't stop it. "It" was a large taco salad, a chocolate shake, and a bag of popcorn she had consumed.

Ray jerked the car to the side of the expressway and stopped, once again threatening to kill the still–spewing Janie. She couldn't stop. Ray opened the driver's door and got out. Through the door opening, he pointed the gun at Janie's head and yelled at her to "Get the hell out of the car!" But, she couldn't move; she wasn't finished emptying her heaving stomach. Cars whooshed past them in a blur, but no one stopped. Passers–by couldn't see

Ray's gun or his soiled clothing. Exasperated, Ray slapped her head and yelled, "OK, bitch, you keep the God–damned car!" He ran off into woods that bordered the expressway, but Janie was unable to raise her head to see where he ran. When she recovered, she drove herself to the police station. Ray was apprehended within a few hours.

As Janie recounted her story on the witness stand, the assembled crowd cheered at her clever crime–fighting saga. I cheered too, but inwardly, judiciously, and all by myself. I learned more from Janie in fifteen minutes than I ever learned in law school. I also learned the importance of a large, fresh, multi–colored taco salad. I think my next book will be a judicial cookbook, <u>Legalese Over Easy</u>.

**For additional copies
Send $20.00 check or
money order to:**

SYMETRY PUBLICATIONS
Box 44177 Cincinnati, Ohio
45244